IF
GOD
ALLOWS

A NOVEL

Robert P. Cohen

Cover and interior design by David Provolo

Paperback
ISBN 978-0-578-21402-3

EPUB
ISBN 978-0-578-43268-7

twitter: @robertpcohen

fb: @robertpcohenwriter

PART 1

CHAPTER 1

My name is Paul Goldberg. I was born and raised in Stonetown, New York. An American suburb as suburban and American as any, populated by men and women who are as New York as New York gets. They fight. They curse. They own landscaping businesses. They're volunteer firefighters, personal trainers, nurses, and hairstylists. They work hard, and they take care of their own. They talk with Italian accents and mannerisms, though few of them actually are Italian. And they party like you've only seen in movies. I've always said that if Scorsese made a film set in the suburbs, he'd base it in a place like Stonetown.

I wasn't entirely like the people I grew up with. Which isn't to say I didn't like them. I loved them. Growing up around them made me who I am today. But I was most definitely the black sheep in town. Or, as my best friends often put it, "A total fucking pussy." Still, the boys always got a kick out of me and liked having me around. Except when they got in fights. When they got in fights I usually spent several days afterward wondering if I had any friends left because I never had their backs in those fights. I like to think that I did have their backs in the spiritual sense—I sent positive thoughts their way and hoped for their well-being. I'd wish from afar for them to win their fights, after I first tried, unsuccessfully, to persuade them against engaging in those fights. I just never wanted to fight, personally.

Things always worked out with time. Some days would pass. They'd miss my jokes, my ability to recount an event in ways that made it seem even better than it was, and my full-throttled enthusiasm for a good party. In turn, I'd miss their equal enthusiasm for a good party, their unwavering loyalty, and most of their jokes. (Though I never liked the jokes that were at the expense of strangers. Those were the jokes that led to fights.)

Rounding out my main circle of friends were a dozen or so young women, half of whom might have been in more fights than any of my male friends. Yes, the women of Stonetown were absolute firecrackers. A tribe of good-time girls with big hearts and short tempers who overdosed on mascara and hair spray for years after it was acceptable to do so. Walking the halls of Stonetown High School always felt like being backstage at the casting of a Mötley Crüe music video. Except for the days when it felt like being backstage at a WWE event.

Most of the girls I dated back then—well, both of them—partied harder than anyone I've met since. First, there was Keri. She said she wanted to be with me because she'd always heard good things from those who knew me best. That I was funny and smart and shit and that I was down for whatever. What really turned her on, she told me, was when she saw me on the back deck of a house party, dancing by myself in the corner to the beat of 2Pac's "Dear Mama." Not dancing well but not giving a shit about how poorly I danced. That's when she grabbed me by the hand and took me behind a dilapidated green shed where we smoked a joint and then made out until our lips swelled.

Keri and I were both virgins when we started dating, but when we had sex five weeks later I was somehow the only one losing my virginity. She attributed it to a combination of strong acid and a free ticket to a Grateful Dead concert. This I found especially infuriating since I was the actual Grateful Dead fan but wasn't allowed to go to the Meadowlands on a school night. She went with her older cousin, Pete, and his friend, the one she ended up sleeping with, because they had a bunch of drugs and an extra ticket and she thought it sounded cool. I asked her not to tell me any further details, other than what the opening song was ("Here Comes Sunshine").

When Keri and I finally had sex, I was pleased to meet my goal of losing my virginity before senior year. It was the night of our junior prom. We'd amassed a stockpile of blow, X, benzos, and ludes, plus a considerable amount of cheap vodka and rum. Typical nineties suburban high school stuff.

Nine couples took three limos out to Montauk and stayed at a two-star motel across the highway from the

9

beach. Just shy of midnight, while our friends went skinny-dipping in the Atlantic, Keri and I slipped away to our room and got undressed without discussion. Keri fell onto the bed, pulling me on top of her, and told me not to put on the condom I was so proud to have purchased. (At Duane Reade, there was a sultry, college-age cashier who I was very happy to make aware of my newfound sexual activity.) Keri said that for my first time I should know what it really felt like to be inside her. It made perfect sense to me so I set the condom on the particleboard nightstand and found my way into her, skin to skin, granting myself that magical revelation every guy encounters when entering a woman for the first time. As the answers to life's deepest mysteries enveloped me like a rip curl, I closed my eyes and imagined having sex with the Duane Reade cashier.

The next morning, I awoke on the beach to a harsh and revealing Montauk sun. I could not recall how I'd gotten there or why I was only wearing underpants but, in retrospect, I was probably lucky to have had on any clothes at all. My eyes gained focus, and I noticed Keri was upside down above a keg of beer, her legs being held by my friends Jamie and Andrew. She was guzzling straight from the tap, which a third friend held to her mouth. I smiled and felt dry, crusted sand fall from my cheeks. Keri was well known as the keg-stand queen of Long Island. Really of Stonetown, but to us it may as well have been the world.

That's my girl, I thought with pride.

Our new bond was palpable, and I felt like a highway to the rest of my life had opened up in front of me. Seeing her there, my soul mate in crime, beer dripping down her forehead as a dozen or so drunk, shirtless teens cheered her on like an Olympian on the verge of breaking a world record, I couldn't wait to have sex with her again.

Upon finishing her keg stand she looked over and saw that I was awake. Smiling with delight she yelled, "Your turn, pussy!" Wondering if she'd slept at all and for how long I had, I asked if I could have some water first. She muttered something about me being such a little bitch sometimes. All of my friends laughed.

After some water and several keg stands each, we went back to the room and had sex again, as we did several times a day for the next two weeks. Then we broke up abruptly for reasons that have never been entirely clear to me. By the start of senior year I was dating her friend Rebecca. It didn't seem to bother Keri at all, and the three of us remained close.

Rebecca was petite and field hockey fit, and we bonded over the game of chess, of all things. We'd play match after match in my room every day after school, and in between she'd thumb through the books on my shelves and we'd talk about some of them and about our dreams and the future. She was the first person I ever knew who did heroin, and I liked the idea of having a girlfriend with that trait. It seemed like something the girlfriend of a poet might do. In fact, I wrote several poems about it, but I never showed them to anyone. Thinking back, it's probably better I didn't.

Every time I asked Rebecca to share her heroin with me she refused, listing various concerns about my future that somehow didn't apply to her own, though I always suspected it had to do with the fact that she only ever beat me in chess after she shot up. She did introduce me to and encourage me to smoke angel dust, which I enjoyed thoroughly.

One day, both of us drunk and high, mid–blow job, she lifted her head and, holding my dick against her cheek, found my eyes with hers.

"Paul," she said.

"Yes, dear?"

"I really don't ever want you to do heroin. But promise me one thing?"

"Anything."

"Whatever you do, if you ever do heroin, like behind my back or something . . . whatever you do, don't do it at the same time as angel dust."

"Okay. I'll promise you that," I said and meant it.

"I love you!" She peppered my shaft with kisses.

"I love you too, dear. But tell me something."

"Fuckin' anything!" She spat on me and began stroking while we talked.

"Should the opportunity ever present itself for me to do heroin and angel dust at the same time, and assuming that I hadn't promised you I wouldn't, why would it be a good idea for me to decline the offer?"

"Good. Fucking. Question," she said.

"I thought so," I said.

"Well . . . because the heroin will make you vomit. And then . . . and then the angel dust will make it feel like you're shitting out of your mouth. It's not a good thing. Trust me."

"Wow. That's serious. I double promise you that I will definitely never, ever do heroin and angel dust at the same time."

"I fucking love you, dude," she said.

"I totally love you too."

"You want me to finish, right?"

"It'd be a lot cooler if you did," I said, referencing a movie we'd watched together several times. She laughed and continued, encouraging me to come in her face.

Later that year, when I told Rebecca that I had been accepted to film school in California, she broke up with me. Even though it was almost six months away, she said she didn't want to delay the inevitable pain. She'd be so sad it would drive her to drink more than usual, so she might as well get started. I was disappointed but didn't argue because she seemed to have a point, and I thought it'd be a good opportunity to practice having sex with other girls before college. I didn't have sex again until the second semester of my freshman year.

CHAPTER 2

"What happened to Wednesday?" I asked no one in particular.

"What's that, mate?" a voice questioned in return.

I had boarded a United Airlines flight out of JFK on Tuesday morning. Three sleeping pills, six glasses of champagne, ten hours of sleep, and a layover in Hong Kong later, I found myself standing groggily in an airport immigrations line in Jakarta on Thursday afternoon. I repeated my question to the only other Westerner in my vicinity, whom I guessed was British but turned out to be Australian.

"Twenty-four hours of flight," I said, "twelve-hour time difference. That puts me in Indonesia Wednesday afternoon. But my phone says it's Thursday. Did I fly through some time warp or something?"

"Funny, mate," he said without laughing.

"Thanks. But really, what happened to Wednesday?"

"Ya must have flown here coming west, right?"

"Right?"

"Well, mate, ya jumped the international date line. This side of the world is roughly half a day ahead. You kinda flew backward from the beginning to the end, if that makes any sense."

"So, I flew into tomorrow?"

"Yup."

"Holy shit. I skipped an entire day."

"Funny, right? So this is your first time in Jakarta, I reckon?"

"Yes . . ."

"You don't know the half of it then. But welcome, welcome. The name's Justin."

"Hey Justin. I'm Paul. Sorry, but all this might take my brain a minute to process."

"No worries. No worries. What brings ya 'bout then?"

"Huh?"

"Why are you here? In Jakarta, mate?"

"Oh. Oh, sorry. I'll be working for an ad agency here."

CHAPTER 3

Working in the advertising industry had not been my original plan. I had first wanted to be a filmmaker. In high school, I had produced several low-budget music videos for some local bands, a short film about a painter who went blind and killed himself, and a comic documentary about social castes in a typical American suburb. I sent copies of my work, along with an ironic video bio of myself, in which I explained why no film school faculty in their right mind would ever want me as a student, to every professor in the film department at the University of Southern California, which was universally regarded as the best film school in the world. In retrospect, I was probably trying too hard to be clever, but by some stroke of luck I received a personal letter from the head of the department not just acknowledging my acceptance but offering me a partial scholarship as well.

"Rest assured, Paul," my favorite section of the letter read, "we haven't discovered and nurtured some of the best filmmakers in the world by remaining within our right minds. We'd be thrilled to have you and your unique brand of visual sarcasm and tension among the great talent in our program."

At USC, a few of my films were well reviewed and widely screened. One of the better of them, a five-minute animated reinterpretation of Pink Floyd's *The Wall*, was told entirely through Lego pieces and figurines, and my favorite professor called it "the most awesomely original thing I've ever seen borne from such an entirely unoriginal, sophomoric, stoner thought." I took it as a compliment.

I followed that up with an experimental piece called *To Me, This Is 17*. Against my favorite professor's advice, I filmed it on Super VHS, because it felt more "of the time." Whatever that meant.

"We have some of the best film production facilities on earth on this campus, and you're going to shoot it on some consumer-quality crap?" my professor asked, rhetorically.

"To me it says 'fuck you,' which is a large part of what *This Is 17* is all about."

"You wanna know what it says to me? It says, 'You're a complete moron who's blowing a last opportunity to make a great impression on faculty and esteemed alumni and one or two Hollywood legends.' But who am I to say? Oh, right. I'm the guy who taught all of them how to make films."

At the senior class screening, my short was viewed

first because it required a different projector than the others. They were all shot on 16 mm film. Since the faculty didn't want to break any momentum by switching projectors midway through, it was decided that mine would open the show unprefaced. Then, while the department dean gave his opening remarks, they would make the switch.

Promptly at 7:00 p.m., as the last of the guests were making their way to the few empty seats left in the theater, the lights went down, and the room got dark. I had purposely left the first seventeen seconds of the video black, for conceptual tension—I knew that no one would register it in the moment, but I wanted to leave something for people to find years later when they studied my early work. Then, what seemed to be a moment of film burning through the darkness turned out to be an actual fire set to the black foam board on which I had the camera focused. As the burning board collapsed in flames, the camera pushed through and the Venice Beach skate park materialized. An attractive blond seventeen-year-old girl walked into focus and pulled off the white, sweat-stained tank top she had on. A hand came onto screen to carve into her abdomen, with an ivory handled straight razor, the lettering, "T-o m-e, T-h-i-s I-s 1-7."

As the sweat-diluted blood dripped down her young skin, the scene dissolved to a grand shot of the Pacific Ocean. Two surfers sat on their boards, waiting for the swells to build. They spoke in stereotypical, early nineties California surfer-speak about existential threats to mankind. The camera circled around them smoothly, almost as if on a track. This had taken me just over thirty takes to perfect from the back of a Jet Ski that I had rigged with side floats and forty-five-pound plates borrowed from Muscle Beach. I had held the camera in a homemade contraption of half-inch framing and bungee cord, creating the effect of a Steadicam with slightly more give and fluidity. The actors hadn't been happy about the myriad extended takes, but these are the things we do for art, I'd explained to them.

Just as the camera stopped circling, the surfers gave each other a quizzical look, broke into laughter, and their accents morphed from California cool to Brooklyn tough. It turned out they were mocking those who were hopelessly concerned with the woes of the world. They scorned liberal smugness and naivete. Finally, seemingly from out of nowhere, two beautiful girls paddled up alongside them on longboards, each carrying a Styrofoam cooler full of Crazy Horse malt liquor. Pink Floyd's "Two Suns in the Sunset" faded in, and the video cut through a soft-paced montage of them all drinking and smoking, touching and kissing. The scene cut wider as the sun set and the sky turned a perfect California gold. Slivers of clouds sliced the glowing, pink highlights. As the surf picked up, the foursome paddled hard simultaneously to catch the same wave. The sea crested, they wiped out, swept under the ocean's unforgiving palm. Quick, frenetic cuts of surfboards and crashing water. Body parts tumbled violently in the sea foam. Flashes of skaters shredding up the skate ramps. Surfers. Waves. Skaters. Surfers. Setting sun. Waves. Mouths gasping for air. Flailing limbs. Broken surfboards. Skaters flying off the ramp. Surfers. Skaters. Borrowed footage of an orca devouring a great white. Waves. Flailing. Gasping. Dead crabs on the beach. Tumbling. Sea foam splashing through the air. Hands. Feet. Surfboards. Skateboards. Total chaos as the song's crescendo played out until the acoustic guitar took over again, and we returned to the same shot from the beginning of the film. The saxophone came in, and the camera tilted into the pit of the skate ramp, revealing the girl from earlier. She had on her shirt again. Blood seeped through where the film title had been cut into her skin. She was now on her back, smoking a joint, staring up at the sky with melancholy eyes. The sound faded to mute. Shadows of skaters brushed her face, and the final credits rolled over the scene through an empty silence.

It would be discussed and questioned, with great speculation among my fellow film students, how I achieved some of those shots. What they would never know was that my friend Andrew's cousin, also from Stonetown, was a Southern California construction tycoon and my film's secret backer. After a phone call from

Andrew and then a screening of some of my early work during an all-night bender at a crack dealer's home in Compton, Bruno Albano was in. He agreed to provide me with three Jet Skis, a forklift, and a seventy-five-foot industrial crane. He would also arrange the permits necessary to use all of the above equipment on a small section of the beach and boardwalk within a four-day period, Monday through Thursday, in late February when the area was least crowded. As an added bonus, Benji, the crack dealer and party host, supplied me with an endless high for the entire four days and half a dozen day laborers from East LA in exchange for a producer credit, full access to hang around the set, and a promise that I would direct his first music video for cost if he ever got his rap album recorded. He never did.

When the audience realized it was safe to react, most of the film students and several of the celebrity guests stood in applause. I remember hearing a few whistles, which made me smile, even if I was irrationally disappointed that it wasn't a full standing ovation.

I stayed for the other films, many of which were mediocre and some of which were great. Closing the show was an ambitious if manipulative war short by a classmate named Danny Allen. Visually, the film was an overwhelming display of stunts and pyrotechnics all crammed into twelve minutes and forty-two seconds, the last two minutes of which featured the main character getting the girl. I found this to be an especially cheap move considering the girl played no other purpose in the film than to be a reward for the hero at the end. Zero character development, no twist, no substance. Just bright lights, quick cuts, what seemed to be a well-budgeted makeup department, and a strangely satisfying extended kiss, followed by one of the worst movie lines I've ever been guilty of falling for in the moment, "Ain't no bombs in the world big enough to drown out the drumbeat of my heart right now." It was a stunning piece of cinematography, I'll admit with a cringe. It was also among the dumbest, most patronizing scripts ever written.

A series of well-polished credits flew in and out of frame to the sound of "Everlong" by the Foo Fighters. The main character and his abruptly introduced love interest walked hand in hand toward the direction of the flames. I knew immediately that Danny would go on to make far more money than I ever would in filmmaking.

I noticed that the two girls seated next to me were crying. I stared at the blond one, who I found especially attractive, wishing my own film could have had that effect on her. She caught me.

"Hey, you're Paul Goldberg, right?" she asked, wiping away a tear with a hint of shame.

"Yes." I wasn't sure whether to be proud of the fact or not.

"That was your film in the beginning? And you did the Pink Floyd Lego film last year, right?"

"Yes." Still not sure whether to be proud of the fact or not.

"I like how your films have so much depth and tension to them. It's amazing. You're super talented."

"Thanks. I tend to favor tension over depth, but I appreciate the sentiment. My films don't make you cry though?"

"Sorry." She allowed herself a small laugh and wiped her eyes again. "Yours really was great, but that last one, I don't know. I mean, I get that it might not have been high art. But it got me. All the intensity. And then that kiss. I imagine them walking through the other side of those flames to have the best sex anyone's ever had. I wish I could find someone like that to walk through flames and make love with."

"I'm not a trained military expert with fire-repellent clothing, but I'd love to make love to you," I replied, shocking myself with the uncharacteristically smooth delivery. "If you'd want to, that is," I added, feeling now more like the bumbling fool I knew myself to be.

"That was pretty cheesy," she answered, "but kind of cute, I guess. And I've been eating these throughout the screening." She took some mushroom caps and stems out of a plastic bag that she'd been gripping and put them in my mouth. I chewed obediently. She added with a coy glance at the floor, "It might be why I'm a little bit horny."

"Oh shit!" I realized, mouth full, "so they probably didn't kick in until after my movie!"

"You're funny."

"I'm serious. You definitely would have cried if your mushrooms were working then. I created the film specifically for that very state of mind."

"Well, they're working now. So, let's go have some fun. I'm Marissa, by the way."

I liked Marissa's attitude and the constellation of freckles that ran from cheek to cheek across the bridge of her nose, so I took her hand and led her out of the row and up the aisle while her friend sat examining a tear she had caught on her fingertip. In the lobby, as we were leaving, my favorite professor caught up with us.

"Mr. Goldberg," he said when our eyes met.

"Hello sir," I replied. "Quite a successful night of cinema, no? Perhaps with the exception of the introductory film?"

"Oh, cut the faux-humble bullshit, Goldberg. It was much better than I expected. To be honest, it was one of the most original and ambitious shitty-quality films I've ever seen. Still should have gone with film over video. Those lens flares would have taken on a much richer spectrum of light. Would have been more emotional. Grittier. And would have looked like an actual art film instead of the world's most creatively produced home video." He gave me a wink and a smile and squeezed my shoulder with pride. "Still," he added, "you might have a future ahead of you yet."

"He was upset I didn't cry for his," Marissa said while hiding her face in my sleeve.

"Sounds about right. But alas, I must go and mingle. You two have a good evening," he said, then lit a filterless cigarette and walked off like a cool, old-school film professor would.

Marissa and I went back to her apartment in Alhambra and did our best to re-create what we imagined postbattle sex would be like. As I was coming, I closed my eyes and pictured myself with the girl from my movie. The one who had the title cut into her smooth, tan abdomen.

CHAPTER 4

"Ad agency, eh? So what agency ya with, mate?" Justin asked.

"MBD Global. Heard of it?"

"Good one! You bastard!"

"Huh?" I was still on cloud nine from barbiturates and the discombobulating effects of time travel.

"Landing the gig at MBD. You must be the new chief creative there, right?"

"Oh, sorry. Yes, that's right. How'd you guess that?"

"Bastard!" He slapped me on the shoulder.

"Is bastard a good thing here?"

"I'm just having a go at ya, mate. Full disclosure, I interviewed for that one myself. Good money agency for Indonesia and the region. Big accounts. Shitty, creatively speaking, but I suppose that's why you're here. Fix 'em all right up, yeah?"

"Sorry about the gig. I guess an American seemed more exotic to them?"

"No worries, mate. No worries. You earned it, I'm sure. What'd you say your name was again?"

"Paul. Paul Goldberg."

"Goldberg? You wouldn't be the Goldberg who did the juice movement, would ya?"

"Guilty."

"Ah, bastard! Ha ha. 'Get juiced!' Good stuff. You get a shipping crate for all the awards on that one? Brilliant, mate!"

"Thanks, man."

"But tell me, on the coattails of a big one like that, you must have had your pick of top jobs. How'd you land here in Jakarta of all places?"

"I want to write a book one day."

"Come again?"

"I want to write a book. A novel. I thought it'd be good material. Jewish born American atheist as top dog at an ad agency in the most Muslim country on earth, which happens to be in Southeast Asia. It's either a novel or a sitcom. Maybe a movie, which I'd direct myself, but a book first."

"Mate. Are you trying to tell me that you took a job on the other side of the world, turned down god-knows-what kinds of offers back home, uprooted your life, all because you wanted to write a book? And maybe make it into a movie one day?"

"Basically."

"You're a madman!"

"Pun intended?"

He screamed in laughter, and I was embarrassed when all of the locals in line stared a concoction of judgment and curiosity at us.

CHAPTER 5

After film school, I tried the Hollywood thing for a while. I worked as a production assistant on a few major films, all of which, I thought, sucked, and I quickly became jaded with the whole scene. I wasn't making enough money to live the way I wanted to live, and I didn't see how that was going to change anytime soon. Then one day I ran into a fellow USC film school alumnus who had graduated the year before I did. He said he was in town visiting from New York City. He lived there now and had been working as a camera operator in commercial production; the work was steady, and the money was good. I remembered seeing his senior film and how average it was. (Come to think of it, his camerawork was inventive, and his lighting applications were more than competent, but his storytelling and overall vision were less than exceptional.) I figured if this guy could do well in the commercial world, there was no reason I couldn't. Hell, if I could hire him as a camera operator, we'd be an unstoppable force.

Soon after that run-in, I moved back to New York, not to Stonetown, but into a small basement studio on the Lower East Side of Manhattan. At the time, it was the cheapest neighborhood you could live in without having to live in Brooklyn. I looked up the top ten ad agencies and sent them copies of my student films with a pathetic cover letter asking for a job. A week later I got a call from one of them about an interview. I wore a cheap suit that I found in a local thrift shop. The HR girl interviewing me laughed and asked why I wore a suit. I told her that I wanted to direct commercials, and she explained to me that directors don't work at ad agencies but there was an opening for an assistant copywriter. She said that the films I had sent her were "interesting," and that I seemed well suited to be a "creative" in the advertising industry.

After meeting with a senior copywriter, who told me about expense accounts and overseas commercial productions, followed by a creative director, who told me to close the door to his forty-eighth-floor corner office so we could get high, I was pretty sure I wanted the job.

I learned quickly that there were two kinds of creatives. There was the kind who tried to make smart, entertaining ads, provoking thought and discussion among the consumer audience, and then there was the kind who made ads the clients wanted (the kind you see on TV on any given day). At the time, the latter seemed to make the most money, and so I decided I'd aim to be one of them.

The ad industry had some great parties, and it was

easy to make a lot of new friends right away. It turned out that I was drawn to the creatives who fought to make clever work. They were always the most compelling people in the room. They had awards for incredibly funny and/or think-piece ads that ran once or twice, late at night on MTV. I admired them and their work, and they seemed to think I was a total fucking hack. But they seemed to like my full-throttled enthusiasm for partying and my extensive use of sarcasm.

One night, five or six years into my career, having come a long way from that first studio apartment, I had a number of industry friends over to my East Village duplex, which overlooked Tompkins Square Park. They had been pestering me to share my student films with them for some time, and my petty side reared its head in wanting to show off the fancy apartment that my hack salary provided. I arranged for three ounces of magic mushrooms and sprinkled it all atop several large pizzas from Joe's on Bleecker Street.

I gathered everyone around my large LED display and gave a short introduction with anecdotes about shit my favorite professor would say. Then I played the Lego film, which was well received. I was overcome with joy to observe that the group was all starting to feel the effects of the mushrooms just as I was hitting play on the next film, *To Me, This Is 17*.

I hadn't watched it in several years, and it was not

at all what I remembered. So many of the choices I had made now seemed questionable, if not pretentious and arrogant. There was so much I could have done better. Script improvements that could have been made. Subtle imperfections in the pacing of the edit. Camera moves and angles. By the time the credits started rolling over Jenny's elusive gaze I was cursing myself for ever thinking I could direct. Cursing myself for being so dumb and brazen as to invite these people, who I held in high regard, over to my home, to show them this piece of crap "film" by which they would soon judge me forever. Encouraged by all of the self-loathing that comes along with the downward spiral of a bad hallucinatory trip, I was tempted to throw my entire entertainment system out of my fifth-floor window. But somehow, my friends all saw it differently than I did.

"Brilliant!"

"Paul, you're actually talented."

"Dude, I had no idea."

"Why? Why don't you put that, what went into that, into your ad work, man?"

I couldn't be sure if they were being polite or actually liked it. But I wanted to feel good about myself and wanted the bad trip to end. I forced myself to believe them. Positive vibes took over, and a grand night of joy, merriment, and the consumption of vast substances resumed.

From that night forward, they still called me "hack," but they delivered it in a more ironic, endearing tone, which I enjoyed. They also shook their heads and laughed whenever I'd tell them which new lowbrow, high-budget commercial was one that I had written. Until the juice movement, that is. That changed everything.

A client with whom I had built a close working relationship had just been promoted to chief marketing officer at a major juice company. They made all of the juices. Orange, apple, pineapple, mango, guava, you name it. If it came from a fruit they put it in a bottle and sold it. But they had been experiencing some backlash recently about the sugar in their juice. There were debates about whether or not kids should be drinking it. Obviously, he couldn't have that.

"We need to flip this shit, Paul. Juice is the original energy drink. The fucking cavemen were squeezing liquid out of fruit and chasing down dinosaurs, damn it."

"You're right. Maybe we should start a movement to rechampion juice. Something beyond just advertising."

"I love that. A movement. That'd be huge. And some sort of rallying cry that the kids can get behind. A catchphrase of some sort."

"Like 'Get juiced'?"

"That's brilliant."

"Really? I don't know. It's just a first thought. Maybe I should think about it more."

"Fuck that, Paul. Go with your gut. Get juiced. I love it. That's it. Can you do something with it?"

"Of course. As soon as I sober up in the morning."

The juice movement was an instant hit. People were talking about it on the news. "Get Juiced" T-shirts and baseball caps were all over college campuses. One of the Beastie Boys appeared at a televised benefit concert wearing a "Get Juiced" button on his denim jacket.

There were industry awards. There was a promotion. There was a generous bonus. There were job offers. I was on the verge of having everything anyone could want. One offer from a large entertainment conglomerate involved two commas and stock options. But, as tempted as I was by the money, I wanted more. I wanted something to write about.

CHAPTER 6

After close to two hours and some insightful, if sleepy, conversation, I made it through immigration, collected my luggage, and said goodbye to Justin. He gave me his business card—Senior Creative Director at Saatchi & Saatchi, Indonesia—and told me to call him to get some drinks and "tour the dark back side of Jakarta" sometime. I said I would, and I meant it.

There was a line of drivers yelling, "You! Taxi, you! Mister! Taxi!" as soon as I walked out of the customs area. I realized I had never confirmed with the agency about where I'd be staying, and I had no idea where to tell a driver to go. My initial sputtering of "downtown Jakarta" earned me a confused look.

"Can you just take me to a nice hotel in an area for tourists?" I asked one taxi driver who appealed to me by being the least aggressive of the gang.

"Ah, you want hotel good for Bule?" he asked.

"Bule?"

"Bule. Is you. You from?"

"New York."

"Ah, New York . . . America?"

"That's the one."

"Yes. I think many Bule stay Four Season. The very much money. Good you."

"There's a Four Seasons?" I was awash with delight. "Please take me there."

"You reservation Four Season?" he inquired, as if it mattered to him.

"No. I only know it exists because you just told me. I have a credit card though."

"Okay," he considered me. "We go. Not far."

The next hour and forty-five minutes was spent inching along in belching, smog-drenched congestion. At traffic lights, paupers pushed their bottles of water and coconuts for sale through the car window. One young child wanted to sell me a pinwheel. I rolled the window down and was smacked by thick diesel fumes and the smells of assorted fried street foods. I had no local currency on me so I made the novice mistake of handing him a five-dollar bill. He said, "Thank you, Mr. Bule," handed me the pinwheel, and ran off. As soon as the others saw this they swarmed the car like pigeons to a loaf's worth of stale bread crumbs. I looked in my wallet and found only hundred-dollar bills. I didn't suppose they'd be able to break one so I rolled my window up. I felt like a piece of shit, but I didn't know what else to do. They banged on my window and pleaded. My driver clicked his tongue at me in the mirror. I wasn't sure if he was judging me for trying to ignore them or for having given money to the one kid in the first place. As we made it to the other side of the intersection the people began to peel off, some working their way to the cars behind ours, others taking a seat on the curb.

The Jakarta Four Seasons was mostly what you'd expect but not quite as nice as the only other one I'd been at, in Buenos Aires. I'd stayed there while making a commercial for an irritable bowel syndrome medication. I had fond memories of that production and that hotel in particular. During the month there I had a fling with the main character of the commercial, whose role was to show how IBS couldn't stop her from having an exciting life, thanks to this medication. She was far out of my league, but circumstances worked in my favor. The head client, the commercial's director, and my creative director were all blatantly competing for her favor right there in the terminal before our trip had even begun. As luck would have it, she and I were assigned adjacent business class seats. Somewhere in between some good laughs and a lot of booze she leaned over and kissed me.

"I can tell already you're the only one who won't spend the month trying to fuck me," she said.

Two years later, she was the star of a hit TV drama and so, even though our affair happened prior to her fame, it did provide for a stabilizing ego boost during times of self-dissatisfaction.

A front desk attendant told me that since I didn't

have a reservation, the best they could give me was a room with two single beds. I could hardly argue, so I gave them my American Express card and signed by the X

It was close to 6:00 p.m. when I got to my room, and I was exhausted. I knew that if I took a nap I'd be out for the night and, despite the jet lag, I was excited to explore my new city. I looked at myself in the bathroom mirror and felt soft. I dropped down for fifty push-ups, and after a difficult thirty-five, I got up, shaved, showered.

I made it as far as the hotel bar before I realized how hungry I was. I ordered a cheeseburger and fries and some local beer, which wasn't bad at all. When I finished eating I ordered a Macallan 18 on the rocks and a shot of tequila. I noticed the sound of giggling in a bar seat to my right.

I turned and my eyes met a beautiful brunette with long, dark hair, a soft face, and tropical complexion.

"Where you from?" she asked.

"Me?"

"Yes, Mister Scotch and Tequila Bule."

"Oh, that must be me then. I'm from New York."

"Ah, New York. I love New York." She smiled. She had emphasized the words "I love New York." Her intonation suggested that she was making a joke, but I wasn't sure if I got it or not. I wouldn't have minded ordinarily. The problem, however, was that she was the only girl I'd ever met whose smile made her less attractive. Her face contorted in a way that looked uncomfortable, her tongue jutted out to the left side of her mouth and her eye on that same side compressed itself into a squint.

"You married?" she asked.

"Nope."

"You have girlfriend?"

"Nope."

"You lie?"

"Lie? Why would I lie about that?"

"Dunno. Handsome man. No wife. No girlfriend."

"Oh. Well, first of all, thank you for calling me handsome. But I don't have a wife because I'm only twenty-eight and haven't lived quite enough for myself yet. And I don't have a girlfriend because I really just landed in Jakarta a few hours ago."

"First time Jakarta?"

"Yes. First time."

"I can be girlfriend for you here."

I chuckled to myself, and she smiled. The face again. I had to look away. It was amazing to me that a girl could be as beautiful as she was and then vanquish that beauty with a smile. I thought to myself in headline form: keep it serious, keep her beautiful.

"What your name?" she asked.

"Paul. You?"

"I Dewi."

I ordered another scotch and bought Dewi a Corona, her apparent drink of choice.

"After twelve Coronas I dance on table," she said, giggling with a wink.

"Well, eleven more to go then."

"No, nine. I have two before you."

She laughed, and I looked up to take stock of the bar's liquor collection.

"You like dance?" she asked.

"Who doesn't?"

"Who?"

"Yes, I like dance."

"Oh. We go dance?"

"Sure. You know a good place to dance?"

"Dragonfly. Best place. Very fancy."

After half an hour in a taxi we pulled into a driveway and security checkpoint that couldn't have been more than a few blocks from the hotel. I was positive we could have walked it in ten minutes. Maybe less.

Dragonfly was what I expected of a club in any major metropolis, and so it surprised me. The difference, though, according to Dewi, was that every single girl in the room, other than herself, was a prostitute. Which made me worry that Dewi might be a prostitute.

I forgot all worries and most thoughts when she pulled me on the dance floor and grinded against me. She had a sultry way about her. I held her ass as she moved it to the beat. It was firm and small, but there was enough of it there to grip, and it turned me on. She pulled away to look up at me, and when I couldn't help but appreciate how attractive she was I made the mistake of smiling at her. Sensing movement in the corner of her lips I pulled her in close to me, trying to give the sentiment of an intimate embrace rather than an attempt to avoid the sight of her widening grin.

She was on Corona number seven when we left Dragonfly. No tables had been danced upon. We got in a taxi, and I told her I'd drop her off before I went back to my hotel. She told the driver her address and then turned to whisper in my ear. "Or I go hotel with you. You want?" She wasn't smiling. She was dead serious and centerfold sexy.

"Yes," I said. Then to the driver, "Four Seasons, please."

Twenty-three minutes and a few blocks later we were at the security check at my hotel.

"Traffic's great at two a.m., huh?"

"Yes. Jakarta," she said. I was glad she didn't get the sarcasm.

When we walked into my room, Dewi noticed the two beds, and her eyes darted toward me with concern.

"Who you stay with?"

"Oh. The two beds? No, don't worry. It's the only room they had. But at least we each get one bed to sleep in."

"You don't want sleep same bed with me?"

I explained that I was kidding, and she laughed. I turned the lights down as dim as they'd go without the room turning completely black.

As I kissed her she turned around to let me unzip her dress. I wished I'd left the lights on for this part, but

I could make out just enough to know that I'd struck gold. Her body was long, and I explored every inch of it as we worked our way to the bed that my luggage was not sprawled across. I reached over, grabbed a condom from my carry-on, put it on, and worked myself inside of her.

She moaned softly. I thought I heard a word but I couldn't make out what it was. I wondered if she was trying to say my name but had it wrong. I tried to ignore it. Picking up the pace, our rhythm built as her indiscernible utterances became slightly more discernible. Is she screaming what I think she's screaming? I thought. Couldn't be. Could it? It could.

She was screaming out for god. But, unlike any of the handful of women I had been with before, she was screaming out for a very specific god. Not the generic god for which almost every girl at one point screams during sex in porn films. Not the god of the West. Not the god as portrayed by the likes of George Burns and Morgan Freeman. She was screaming for *her* god. The god of over two hundred million Indonesians and another billion beyond. The god of Cat Stevens and Muhammad Ali. She was screaming, "Allah! Allah! Oh, Allah!"

CHAPTER 7

On my ninth day in Jakarta I woke up early. I had a massive hangover, the residual effect of eight days of drinking and screwing. I'd been to almost every bar and club in the city and had had sex with seven of the most beautiful women I'd ever had sex with, one of whom was only beautiful when not smiling. What was not helping my hangover at the moment were the calls to prayer blaring through my skull, transmitting pure dissonance from the thousands of minarets posted around the city, as occurred five times a day, every day, without fail.

The week had been a tornado of prayer and sin. As women would scream to their lord from my bed, the city would punctuate it all with exclamations to the heavens. It was strangely unsettling, but I liked the unholy idea of it: these Muslim women in their Muslim nation calling to their god while simultaneously breaking their bond with him. All of this punctuated by a reminder of that very god's presence as blasted through 1950s-era, treble-heavy surround sound.

I walked through the hotel lobby looking for my

new executive driver, Rahim, who I had been told would meet me there. I realized I'd have no way of telling him apart from the other local men who eagerly stood around the lobby, but one of the bellhops approached me to let me know that Rahim was waiting curbside. I tipped him one hundred thousand rupiah and made my way to the exit. As soon as I stepped outside a man scurried from a small black SUV, running toward me, waving.

"Mr. Paul. Hello, Mr. Paul. I Rahim. Sorry. I think maybe no good I come in hotel. Very nice hotel. Very expensive."

"Jovial" is the word that springs to mind when I think of Rahim. I'd have guessed he was thirty-five at most, but one of those thirty-fives that could have been twenty-three or forty-four. We shook hands, and he bowed his head. I was pretty sure that Indonesians weren't the bowing kind of Asians, but I returned the bow anyway, if half-heartedly.

I was about to open the door to the passenger side when I saw he already had the back door opened for me. He smiled, and I shrugged in concession and got in. From the moment we pulled past the security check at the hotel's exit we were ensconced in thick, unmoving traffic.

"This traffic really sucks, huh, Rahim? About how far to the office?"

"Not far, Mr. Paul. Maybe two kilometer. Maybe forty or fifty minute. No more though." Then, the be-all and end-all in explaining local traffic patterns: "Jakarta."

After a few minutes of getting not much conversation out of Rahim I asked if he had any music.

"You know the Iron Maiden?" he asked.

"Excuse me?"

"Ah. Sorry. Maybe you no like. I have one tape. The Iron Maiden. From British I think. The heavy metal."

"Dude. Iron Maiden. Which tape do you have?"

He held up an unlabeled cassette tape and looked to my eyes in the rearview mirror, awaiting approval. Someone must have dubbed the album for him. It didn't matter to me where it came from. Iron Maiden brought back such pleasant memories of my youth, and just hearing the name gave me a strange anchor to home while sitting there in a river of smog, on the other side of the world, being passed en route to my new advertising agency by a man walking his donkey while roosters scurried out of the way.

"Please, Rahim. Let's listen."

"Yes, Mr. Paul. Very good," he answered proudly.

"Mr. Paul. Mr. Paul, you sleep? We here. The office."

"What time is it?"

Rahim held his phone up to allow me to read the time display. It read 9:24 a.m. Groggy eyed, I looked around at a mostly empty parking lot.

"Looks pretty grim," I said.

"Many people come soon. Traffic. Jakarta."

My office was nothing to write home about, but it was perfectly functional insofar as it had walls, a ceiling, and a door. There was also an adequate window and a couch, the latter of which would suit my post-lunch naps just fine.

I sat at my desk and leaned back in my seat. It would do, I thought. It would do just fine. There was a new MacBook Pro and some pens in a penholder, along with a branded MBD stationary pad. I took a pen from the holder and wrote on the pad:

- *Buy local map.*

- *Write thank-you letters to governmental urban planners in NYC and LA — They are underappreciated!*

- *Workout.*

I turned in my chair, looked out the window, and noticed my view was as harsh a contrast as one could find from that of my previous office on the forty-seventh floor of a midtown Manhattan skyscraper. My third-story view, across what I interpreted to be a moat, revealed a small village. It was as if my window frame were a large-screen TV and the scene I stared at was a Sally Struthers Save the Children commercial. Pillars of smoke wafted from behind a grouping of tin-roofed huts that formed a lazy circle in the center of the village. Off to one edge of the circle, a group of kids were kicking some unidentifiable object around a dusty patch of dirt. On the opposite edge of the circle, a shirtless man was banging a thick stick against another. After several minutes of this, no visible progress had been made, and I couldn't determine a purpose for the action. There was no recognizable survival goal that could have been attributed to his effort. It's possible there was no purpose at all and the action was for its own sake. Perhaps, I thought, he was a village Zen master of some sort. This could have been his unique brand of meditation. I laughed to myself that one could make a killing in a hip Manhattan spa, promoting stick striking as the next new age meditational trend.

Lost in a thought spiral, I imagined myself in an alternate universe, the product of a different sperm finding its way to the egg of this man's mother. In what world could I have been him? Would I have passed my days in similar fashion, content in my hut village? Would any stimulus have given me a spark of a wish to find something beyond what I had in front of me at any given time? Would I have had the slightest inkling of a thought about how satisfying it felt to trade one's frequent flier miles in for a first class ticket to Lisbon on a whim? Maybe nothing would be different at all except for opportunity and sanitation.

"I see you've already put your pen to great use," a female voice broke through my daydream.

I turned to find a twentysomething woman standing in front of my desk, covering a giggle with her hand. She had a cute, round face with short, curly hair and dimples so deep and adorable you'd want to eat cereal out of them. She wore a simple, long-sleeve white sweater and a conservative-length skirt that revealed an attractive, slightly thick shape. Her eyes conveyed kindness and welcome. She looked down at my pad and back up to me.

"What?" was all I could think to say in the moment.

"I'm sorry. I didn't want to disturb you," she said. "You seemed focused on the window and I glanced down at the desk and . . . I'm sorry. I'm Nisa." She put out her hand to shake mine, and I stood and met the gesture with my hand and a smile.

"Hi, Nisa. I'm Paul. Do you work in the creative department?"

"Yes, I guessed you were Paul. Because you are the only strange white man here."

"Fair enough."

"I should tell you the truth, that I Googled you and your juice movement. Which was so very interesting. The way you created something so much bigger than just a commercial with the 'Get Juiced' phrase. So, I knew you were Paul. I saw your picture. Apparently, you were in the news. A big shot in America, maybe? Anyway . . . Paul. I am Nisa. Your new assistant. Nice to meet you."

"Hi Nisa. I was only big in the ad industry, if at all. Don't let it fool you. You're quite a talker, aren't you?"

"Do you mean this in a good way or a bad way? I am known for being very friendly. But it is a good thing for you. I'm very well liked. So, when you have to tell someone to do something, I can help."

"It was a neutral observation, really. Most people here have fairly short replies. I assumed it was a language thing."

"Oh, it is. My English is very good. I studied international communications at the University of Melbourne. I also minored in Western literature, for your information. Many other people here speak English but maybe not so good."

"Well, if there's one person who speaks English so well, I'm glad it's you. So, Western lit, huh?"

"Correct."

"Cool. We'll have to compare notes one day."

"I'd like that."

"What time do things get started around here?"

"It's supposed to be nine thirty. But usually more like ten. Sometimes ten thirty or eleven for some people."

"Eleven a.m. or p.m.?"

She laughed before explaining, "Some people come from far. And the traffic . . . Jakarta."

"I've heard that a lot. But if there's always traffic, don't people know to leave earlier in order to be on time?"

"Soon, Paul, you will understand the ways here. Some things will be very strange to you, I think."

"Some things are already very strange to me."

"Are you married?"

"Is everyone going to ask me that?"

"In Jakarta, yes. In the office, no, they will ask me. What shall I say?"

"I'm not married. I'm only twenty-eight, you know."

"Yes, I know. Very young for a chief creative officer. But old not to be married. Girlfriend?"

"Nope."

"Okay."

"You're not gonna ask if I'm lying?"

"No. Should I?"

"No, of course not."

"I already knew that you weren't."

"So are you married? Or boyfriend?"

"Not exactly. Is there anything you'll need or anything you'd like me to do for you today?"

"I'd love to meet the department, like, as a group, when they're all in. So, maybe after lunch, say, around seven p.m."

"Very funny, Paul. I'll have the department gather before lunch at eleven thirty for an informal welcome. The other department heads have asked to take you to lunch. I'll arrange that for twelve thirty?"

"Yes, please do. Will it actually happen at twelve thirty?"

"Inshallah."

"A prayer?"

"It means, basically, if it is god's will. We acknowledge that things are out of our control."

"So if god allows, it will happen? And if something doesn't happen, it wasn't his will?"

"Correct."

"Very convenient."

"I sit right outside your office there, Paul. So feel free to tell me if you need anything."

"Why do you call me Paul when everyone else says 'Mr. Paul'?"

"Would you prefer if I call you Mr. Paul?"

"Not really. No. Call me what you like."

"Okay. I'm happy to meet you, Paul. And happy you're here. I think this will be great for us. And for you."

"Inshallah?"

"You are catching on now, Mr. Paul."

She left the room and closed the door. I turned back to the window. The kids had drifted closer to the man with the sticks. He yelled something and lifted one stick above his head in a manner meant to threaten. They ran off laughing, and he resumed his act. Stick struck stick beneath the will of man.

CHAPTER 8

Earlier in the week, about four days after I'd arrived in Jakarta and six days after I'd left New York, I'd called Justin.

He answered, "Mate! Or should I say 'Dude'?"

"I'm growing fond of 'mate.'"

"Great! So how ya holding up, mate?"

"Not bad, actually. Sorry I haven't called sooner, considering you're my only friend in Asia. I got a little distracted."

"Ha! I knew you'd like the women here. Been having fun then?"

"Yes. Definitely. It's a bit of an overload, but it's been enlightening."

"Glad to hear it. Did you start at the agency yet?"

"Next week."

"Perfect. Well, whatd'ya say we share some tales over beer tonight. Some of the other expats'll be out. You can meet the gang."

"Cool. I've always wanted to be part of an expat gang of friends. Total *Moveable Feast*. Good material."

"Mate, you are too funny. Where ya staying?"

"The Four Seasons."

"Well damn. That CCO money must be all right."

"By Indonesian standards, I suppose."

"Ha ha. In that case, drinks on you. Grab you in front of your lobby at eight?"

"See ya then . . . mate," I said.

I walked outside a few minutes before eight and sat on the steps in front of the hotel.

Justin sent a text that read, "5 mins away. Major traffic mate. When will I learn, right?"

I got up and walked into the hotel bar. My favorite bartender was working, and I smiled at him. His face was aglow to see me.

"Ah, good evening, Mr. Paul. A beer you? Whiskey?"

"No, Deni. I'm pretty exhausted. I'm thinking to have a Red Bull and vodka."

"Ah. Another late night, Mr. Paul?"

"You could say that."

"Would you like the very good vodka, Mr. Paul?"

"Yes. A lot of it. But a lot of Red Bull too."

I drank the glass down in one slow, steady motion while Deni stood staring, wide grinned. I asked for my bill, and when I walked back to the front of the hotel Justin was there waiting in the back seat of an SUV.

Eventually, we pulled into a small parking lot and a man, who didn't seem to be assigned in any official capacity to such a task, helped guide us into a parking spot in which a toddler could have parked a tractor trailer.

"Good thing that guy's here to help us park," I said.

"Yeah. It's an enterprising little activity here. Guys find an unclaimed parking

lot and delegate themselves as attendants. They work for tips. Can't knock 'em, right."

"Respectable enough. I'll give the entrepreneurial spirit some credit."

Justin's driver tipped the guy a ten-thousand-rupiah note, and I did the same, just to feel like I was in on local things.

We walked into a bar called Star Deli, and it was set up like an American-style country pub with local waitresses wearing outfits inspired by those of the Dallas Cowboys cheerleaders. Several of them rushed over as soon as they saw Justin.

"Hello, Justin. Welcome back."

"You bring present for me?"

"Hi hi, Justin. You bring new friend?"

"Ah, yes, of course. Ladies, this is my new friend, Paul. He's from America," Justin said.

"America? Well, hello, Mr. Paul. Welcome from Star Deli," one of them said.

After greeting them all and taking in some very suggestive glances, I ordered "the best local beer available" and turned to Justin. "So, why is it that I'm Mr. Paul and you're just Justin?"

"Ah, mate. It's just a respect thing here. Once you have sex with them you'll be Paul. Maybe sooner."

"Good to know. So then, it's not just me? Having an easier time than is normal . . . with the ladies and all?"

"No, mate. You just happened to land in the greatest place on earth for a single man."

"I sensed something was up. It's been an amazing few days."

"Right? And the thing is, it's not just that they're easy to get. They're very good at it too. Sex."

"I have noticed they're pretty orgasmic."

"Are you kidding? Women here have their first orgasm before the last button is undone."

"That's pretty good, Justin. You must be a writer."

"I appreciate that, mate. But it's true."

"So I'm learning."

Our drinks arrived amid a sea of smiles and awkwardly flirtatious gestures. We toasted to good times ahead and took a seat in a booth with a few of Justin's friends who had just arrived. One of them, David, I guessed was Australian but was actually British. There was another guy from France, named Philippe, and one more from Michigan, named Scotty. Scotty was a geologist, consulting for an American oil company.

"What up, New York!" Scotty exclaimed with an exuberance that I predicted could get annoying very quickly.

To break the ice, I asked, "Should I call you Michigan, or is Scotty okay?"

"Yeah, Scotty'll do fine. How long you here?"

"Well, a few days so far, but I'll be here indefinitely."

"He's the head creative honcho at one of the biggest agencies in town," Justin chimed in on my behalf. "Could have had his pick of jobs in the world, but he's come to our little paradise to write the great novel of the new millennium."

"Is that right, New York?"

"Well, I never said it was going to be great." Everyone laughed and more drinks arrived. About four or five beers in, I noticed Scotty addressing the waitresses in a lewd manner.

Now, I understood that I was in a place with different male-female relationship dynamics than I was used to. Sex was available for those who wanted it. Romance and chivalry did not seem to be the price of admission. But I didn't think anyone needed to be a dickhead about it. Even in Stonetown, where men would hurl insults at one another like high-velocity dodgeballs, no one ever found pleasure in verbally degrading women. At least not to their faces. Scotty was the American I'd always heard about but never realized existed in reality. He was a total and complete prick.

"New York, my man. I'm out of here," he finally said to my great relief. "Have to catch a chopper out to some island in the morning. Can't be too hungover. Explosives testing and shit like that. But hey, we gotta exchange numbers and hang. We'll terrorize this town. Double team some whores for Allah." Somewhere in his choice of words were explanations to multiple geopolitical concerns, I was sure of it.

"Yeah, Scotty. That'd be fucking delightful," I offered with the least bewildered smile I could muster.

"New York. You're a riot, man," he said, handing me his business card: Scott Cantrell, Regional Director of Geological Programming, Asia-Pacific. Energy Consulting Corp.

I assured him I'd call, positive I wouldn't. On his way out he made sure to touch inappropriately every Star Deli waitress within reach. Approaching the door, he turned back to the table. "Yo, Justin! You gotta introduce him to Jeff. Jeff's gonna love him! Peace, guys!" Then he lifted a peace sign to us and walked out.

"So, that's Scotty, huh?" I turned to the guys.

"Quite the character, wouldn't you say, Paul?" I could sense Philippe feeling me out.

"To be honest with you," I answered, "I don't mean to insult your friend or anything like that, but he seemed like an absolute dickface." They all looked at one another and burst into laughter.

After a few more drinks and several good, extended laughs, Philippe and David both had to go home to their wives. I was tempted to call it a night as well, but Justin insisted we go to a place called Tabac.

"It's very New York City, mate. You'll love it. Plus you should meet Jeff."

"He's not another Scotty, is he?"

"Ha. No, mate. Promise. Cross my heart."

"Well, in that case . . ."

While Justin's driver took us on a shortcut through the back roads of the city and Justin texted away on his phone, I observed the scenes out my window. The underbelly of Jakarta at night was straight out of a spy movie. Countless alleys and dark, mysterious passageways. People gathered in shadows, allowing me to imagine dealings of local and international intrigue. The narrow corridors were just wide enough for our SUV to scrape its way between the high cement walls, and neither the driver nor Justin seemed to mind the occasional sparks as we sped through. I was picturing cinematic chase scenes, villainous ambushes. It were as if a fictional world manifested itself in real life. I finally felt the sensation of living the novel I'd always wanted to write. I was a part of it, in it. There was a palpable sense of place and of great potential for experience. I hoped I'd remember it all in the morning so that I might write it down for later use.

The entrance to Tabac was a secret panel through a coffee shop's 1930s-era phone booth. I was reminded of a small bar in the East Village where I used to go for bespoke cocktails. Stepping through, I was surprised to find a large room, more reminiscent of a Los Angeles lounge. The design was hip and modern but regal. It was an impressive venue, and it made me realize that Jakarta would never cease to surprise me. At the bar, Justin asked what I wanted to drink. I said I'd have a beer, but then I looked up at the bar and ten thousand volts of pleasant surprise rushed through me when I noticed, on a mirrored shelf above the register, a bottle of fine Kentucky bourbon, the label for which hosted the portrait of a warm and affable old man known as Pappy.

"I'll have a Pappy Van Winkle. Is that a twenty-year I see?"

"Yes, sir," said the bartender. "You would like some? Very good. Very expensive."

"Two, please. Neat, no ice."

"Yes, sir. I know neat, no ice." He smiled a smile I couldn't interpret and reached for the bottle.

"So that's good stuff or something?" inquired Justin.

"Well, the twenty-three-year is like liquid gold. But most people couldn't tell the difference. To be honest, I'm one of them. Twenty or twenty-three, it's damn good stuff. Very hard to find. I can't believe they have it here, of all places."

"Yeah, well, it's Jeff's place. I'm sure he smuggles it in from wherever they make it. He's a resourceful number," Justin said.

When our drinks arrived I handed one to Justin, and we clinked glasses.

"To your new home, mate," he said.

"To new friends," I offered in return. I always thought there were few better ways to bond with another man than through expensive brown liquor.

Justin excused himself to visit the bathroom, and I took in the atmosphere. From certain angles I did feel like I was back home. Some hybrid between New York and LA and maybe some other place that doesn't really exist except in the minds of those who have read far too many hipster novels. I turned to the bar to ask for another Pappy. "Make it a double this time."

"Expensive taste, New York," a voice came from behind me.

I prayed that it wasn't Scotty, though the accent was definitely more New York than Michigan.

"You from New York as well?" I turned and asked.

"Hey man. I'm Jeff. Justin told me there was a New Yorker over here I had to meet." He reached out his hand to shake mine.

"Ah, the infamous Jeff. Nice to meet you," I said, offering my hand in return.

"Yeah, dude. Justin says you're good people. Kinda like our boy Scotty." He gave me the look that New Yorkers always give each other to accompany a sarcastic statement. In context, I took it as if a mark of the Masons. He was one of us.

We both laughed, clearly on the same page regarding the Scotty issue.

"This is a nice little place you have here, Jeff. Love the fine bourbon option."

"Thanks, man. I'm just glad you appreciate that. Not many order it. Which is good 'cause the shit is hard to get. But those who do, I always know they're on the level."

"How'd you end up as a nightlife entrepreneur here of all places?"

"Same as you, man. The ad game. My ex-wife and I started a production company out here. Now it's hers. I got to keep the bars. We did these as side projects in between productions. Mostly recycling materials from our commercial sets and shit like that."

"Resourceful. And it sounds like you got the better half of the split. Bars plural, you say?"

"Yeah. I've been at it for a while. I got this place. A spot in Bali. And minor partnerships in spots in Thailand and Moscow. You ever go to the Tunnel?"

"In New York?" I asked.

"Yeah. I was in on that one. Designed the fixtures and everything. After doing some cool bars for a bunch of films, I realized some of them should be real, ya know? Made some opportunities for myself. You end up meeting some major fucking characters in the club scene when you're the one opening the clubs. Some good times. You know Coffee Shop in Union Square?"

"Yeah, I used to brainstorm ad ideas there and gawk at all the models."

"I was part of that too, man. You know the phone booths toward the back?"

"Vaguely."

"I had some street kids rip those right out of the fucking streets in Brazil. *City of God*–type shit. Smuggled 'em up to New York in olive crates."

"They grow olives in Brazil?" I asked.

"Who the fuck knows?"

"Fair enough. You'd make a great terrorist."

"That's funny. Probably good money though." We both laughed, and he told the bartender to top off my drink. Justin came by with a statuesque local girl on his arm.

"Well, mates," Justin said, "glad you gents could meet. I'd stay and hang out, but this young lady and I have some unfinished business to get to." She tugged at his arm while smiling at Jeff and me. "You boys don't get into too much trouble. I've got that part covered . . ." he trailed off as she pulled him toward the door.

"Not bad," I commented to Jeff, a little bit jealous of the night Justin was about to have.

"Hooker," Jeff said.

"What?"

"Not a cheap one either."

"Really?"

"Yup."

"I wouldn't have known. How can you tell?"

"You just know it, dude. Especially in my fucking business. You develop an eye for it. Like a taste for fine liquor, right?" We clinked glasses and volleyed travel anecdotes, of which Jeff's were far more interesting. I made mental notes and considered ways to incorporate this experience into my novel.

"Well, my man," Jeff said, "I spy a little elf who has

been laser fucking you with her eyes for the past half hour. And the good news is she ain't no hooker."

I looked over and saw a girl who did seem to have some elfish qualities to her. Her ears were small but stuck out, somewhat sideways, and her chin came to a dramatic point. Still, she was uniquely attractive, and I had an excellent buzz going. Jeff handed me his business card, told me to go have fun and not to be a stranger. I told him we'd talk again soon and meant it.

Petra had a high-pitched voice and a skinny body, and during foreplay, I experienced something I had never known was possible. Not love—it was something she did when I put a finger inside of her. A bewildering, constricting pressure, and then a quick release. I pulled my finger out and looked at her, but her eyes were closed and she continued kissing me. I crept my finger back inside of her, and it happened again. I felt like an intergalactic explorer, spelunking in a space cave that was its own living, breathing organism. I was walking the path of Captain Kirk, studying the carnal intricacies of deep space while improving interplanetary relations. Petra squeezed her vaginal walls against my digit as if she had a third hand lubricated and stationed within her pelvic region. I inserted a second finger and her clamp tightened. With equal fascination and arousal, I varied my finger play, in and out, up and around as she squeezed and released. Even as I'd tease my way around her clitoris and outer labia, her apparatus would bite out at my hand and pull it back in. I put a condom on and dared to put myself inside of her alien contraption as she slowly jerked me off from within. Her pressure pulsed with the rhythm of my thrusts, and if I hadn't been slightly distracted by pondering her biological mechanisms, I'd have come instantly. It felt incredible, but beyond that it *was* incredible. I imagined the things an evolved nation of women could accomplish with such abilities. We reached the point at which she began to scream for her god, and I thought to myself, Yes, maybe he does deserve some credit. Such talent did not seem cultivated. It was given as a gift from something greater. Something beyond my understanding. Something beyond this world.

"Oh my fucking god!" I shouted before reaching full transcendence.

CHAPTER 9

My first significant client meeting was with the regional director of skin care, Southeast Asia, for a global pharmaceutical company. I knew that Indonesia, with a population of more than 220 million, was one of the company's most lucrative markets. Needless to say, impressing this man was important.

The meeting was scheduled for 10:00 a.m., and I arrived at the building at about 9:45 a.m., just as the guitar solo of Iron Maiden's "Wasted Years" was hitting full throttle. Rahim knew that I liked to hear a song in its entirety before turning off the stereo. He pulled just short of the main entrance, and when one of the security guards approached, Rahim said something in Bahasa that got a laugh out of the guard. As soon as the song ended, Rahim hit stop on the tape deck, assuring the next song would be queued for later, and he pulled up a little farther. I would have gotten out and walked the extra twenty feet, but Rahim liked to be a good driver. More so, he wanted other drivers to see him as a good driver. Over the several weeks I'd spent with Rahim, I'd really come to enjoy him. He took pride in his work and was a good, thoughtful soul. I felt like he was above the gossip and status jockeying of the other drivers, but I also understood why it was important to him that he was at least perceived to play within their rules.

Just after 10:30 a.m., the rest of the agency team arrived to find me in the lobby, scribbling notes. I told them I was making meeting notes, but I was working out an angle for my novel that involved me befriending the man in the village next to the office. Earlier that morning he'd been chasing some slum dogs around with a javelin-like pole. I wasn't sure what his purpose had been, which was no different than every other morning. I'd arrive at the office, look out my window, see him performing some inexplicable task, and I'd be tempted to take a walk over and befriend him. Nisa often pleaded against it when I asked her to come as my interpreter.

"Boss, you're from two different worlds. You will have nothing in common."

"We're both men. We have that in common. Just two men trying to find our way in the world."

"But what you are looking for is different than what he is looking for."

"How so?"

"Well, he would like a proper house. With plumbing. And to eat good food every day. A clean shirt or two. A wife and children. And you would like to travel around the world, taking an odd job so that you can fulfill a dream of writing a great American novel. And maybe selling the movie rights."

"I think you mean *the* great American novel. But I never said it would be great. Nor American, for that matter," I snapped back at her, feeling slightly scolded. "But I get your point," I said. "Could just be white man's guilt. Or residual Jewish guilt."

"So it's true that Jews are guilty?"

"Well, as guilty as any religious people. But it's more of a saying. One that stays with you long after your faith has retired."

"I'd like to hear more about that one day."

"What if I bought him a house?" I asked, pretending to ignore what she'd said. "Could we be friends then? What would a modest starter house cost around here?"

"A starter house?" She was incredulous. "I would like to use one of your phrases right now and tell you that you are killing me."

"You're funny sometimes, Nisa."

"You are funny almost all of the time, Paul."

At 11:15 a.m., the agency team and I were escorted into the conference room where we were greeted by the marketing team who were in turn waiting for their boss, Mr. Indra. After summarizing a filtered version of my life story for the room and fielding various questions about being married, having or not having a girlfriend, how much I like Jakarta, and whether or not I was Christian, Indra finally walked in just shy of 11:45 a.m.

"Paul. Very good to meet you. Please forgive my tardy entrance. The traffic here is almost as bad as in Mumbai!" We shook hands like men do when inspecting one another for faults.

"Almost as bad? So I guess I should leave now if I want to visit you there next Ramadan, huh?"

"Ah, Western sarcasm. I don't get much of that here, but I do so enjoy it. You are most welcome, Paul. Shall we begin?"

After my presentation I answered some questions from the group and fielded to my team any that related to local culture. Our managing director, Santi, did a great job of explaining how the creative ideas were relevant to Indonesian insights. As head suit and basically my business counterpart, she came off impressively. And while her exaggerated cleavage was part of what kept people listening to her, the words coming out of her mouth made a lot of sense; they were what I would have said myself if I knew anything about local culture. Ironically, one of the few things that I thought I knew about local culture had something to do with female modesty. Every day I learned that I knew nothing at all.

Indra finally spoke. "I'm very impressed, Santi. Paul, you and the team have managed to hit on some very unique ideas, and I think we have several options here for viable new campaigns."

"Glad to hear it, Indra." I tried never to speak too much once a client signaled positive receipt of the presentation.

"Please allow me some time with the team, and we'll revert back soonest possible with next steps." He spoke like a business e-mail. But his deep Indian accent made it work.

We shook hands with a mutual understanding, and he pulled me aside to chat privately while Santi entertained the rest of the client team.

"Paul, I hope you will be happy here in Jakarta. It's an odd place, but a single man such as yourself can have a great deal of fun. Let's plan to enjoy drinks together very soon." I nodded, and he added, "Not as client and agency but as friends." I smiled and told him I'd count on that.

It was just after 1:00 p.m., and I was hungry, so I offered to buy the team lunch, though only Santi joined me.

"They don't want to eat with the bosses. They cannot be themselves, maybe," Santi offered, seeing my disappointment.

"I see. So, tell me about you," I said.

After a longer biography than I expected, we got to the part in which Santi was a rock and roll groupie.

"Wait, what? Are you serious?"

"Oh, I don't joke about this."

"But aren't you married? And Muslim?"

"Well, I wasn't married at seventeen, Paul. And the other part, we won't discuss."

"Okay. So, like, for example . . . what kind of bands are we talking about here?"

"Let's just say that . . . if Metallica ever came to perform in Jakarta again, the drummer would be very sad to know that I'm married now."

"What? You banged little Lars?"

"He's very big, actually." She covered her mouth as she giggled.

"Well, that figures."

"But enough about me. Very boring story. How about you, Mr. Chief Creative Officer? Why aren't you married?"

"You know, I've never been asked that question as much as I have since moving here," I said. "In fact, I'm not sure I was asked that question at all before moving here."

"I don't think that's an answer. But I can try to explain if you can promise to answer."

"Reluctant as I am, I'll take you up on that."

"I know you may see Indonesia as very liberal," she said. I didn't see it that way at all, but I let her continue. "But we are a very traditional society. Marriage is an important part of that. It's what you're supposed to do. For some, it is not always easy. There is still sometimes the arranged marriage, but it is less often and not easy for those who come from families with less means. So, I think that possibly people look at you, a successful, handsome man, and they wonder, you must have many options. But you choose to remain single. That is a very odd thing for people here. Can you understand?"

"I don't see myself as handsome."

"No? But others do. Not myself, because I am married. But girls in the office say that you are. They say this, Paul."

"Really?" I asked. "Which ones?"

"I cannot say. It would not be professional. But they say it. About your curly hair. You know the blond hair is not very common here. Very exotic for some."

"Exotic?" I blurted out with surprise. "Women in the office see me as exotic?"

"Let's forget the women in the office. Do you not notice attention from women in Jakarta?"

"I do get a lot more attention from women here than I did back home."

"So you are not married because you had no attention from women until now?"

"I didn't say that. I just don't think it had anything to do with how I look. I kind of relied on my wits. And luck, mostly. Though not as much luck as some."

"Perhaps you were less exotic to the women in your country. So maybe now, in Indonesia, you will have an easier time finding a wife. Because they will find you. All you have to do is choose. And if you still do not have the luck, there are ways to help your luck."

"How's that?"

"Oh, very easy. You just hire a *dukun*. Not cheap, but for a man of your means, a very good option."

"I'm not going to marry a prostitute!" I exclaimed with too much volume. Santi's expression turned to shock as the patrons nearby darted glances toward us.

"Paul!" She shrunk down in her seat, embarrassed, but must have read the deep confusion in my face as her expression softened and the other diners went back to their business. "A *dukun* is not a prostitute," she assured me. "It's a witch doctor."

CHAPTER 10

When I first addressed the creative department, I said that they should all visit my office and let me know how I could help them to do better. Aside from all else that was new to me, this was also my first management position. I tried to mimic what I had seen other creative leaders do in the past, but I was also dealing with an entirely different culture. I wondered how my favorite creative leaders from throughout my career would have handled the situation I had put myself in. After much consideration, I realized that none of them would have put themselves in my situation.

The first team I met with was made up of Purwoko and Gita. They were two cool young dudes who seemed like some guys I could relate to.

"How's it going?" I began.

"We were promise the raise," Purwoko replied.

"Excuse me?"

"You want to help things be better. We promise for raise. You help us with money," Gita elaborated for me. I was a little thrown off by the direction the conversation had taken, considering we had barely just said hello. But

I did want to know how I could be of help, and they were responding. I thought it best to humor them, having no ideas how budgets worked yet, who was or wasn't due for a raise, and if there was any protocol or policy set in place for these things.

"Well, gentlemen, I'm sure you both deserve raises, but let's start from the top. Who promised you raises? The last guy who had my job?"

"Yes. And boss before him. They promise, and they lie."

"I hate bosses who lie. But why do you think it never happened, other than the fact that they might have lied?"

"They come and work here only short time. They promise, so we work. Then they leave for new job. Very quick. Then new boss come and says he new. Then later he promise, and later he leave with no raise."

"You see, Mr. Paul," Gita said, "we are promise the raise and don't get. Because the boss all come and go while we stay and work."

"Well, I can see why you would be upset. And like I said, I'm sure you both deserve rewards for your hard work. But . . . well . . . I am new. Let me just figure out how things work around here. Let me talk to the rest of the department and then talk to the board of directors and human resources. If what you're telling me is true, I'll do everything I can. I won't make a promise that it will happen, but I will promise to try hard. And I won't be leaving here anytime soon." I figured it would take me at least a year to gather enough material for a worthy novel. "In the meantime, why don't you tell me what you've been working on?"

As it turned out, they had been working strictly on what many in the industry refer to as scam ads. That is, ads that were never assigned or paid for by an actual client but which could be entered in advertising industry awards shows. This was a common practice in the business and especially popular in Asia for some reason. People loved their awards at any cost.

"You want more money, but you haven't produced any work that makes the agency money. I do believe that if you're promised something you should get it, but this might be part of the problem."

"We make work for award. Very good for agency. Good for us."

"Have you won many awards?" I asked.

"Not yet," Purwoko said.

"Well, here's the truth. The only thing good for the agency is money. The only way for the agency to make money is for our clients to be successful. And the only way for them to be successful is if they have actual, re-al-world advertising that people can understand without too much thought, work that makes these people want to buy the clients' products. Because then, the client makes more money, gives us more money, and I can give you more money. Does that make sense?"

"But the award is very popular."

"True. But, well, let me put it this way. A professor at my film school, he made an art film that won all sorts of awards at film festivals all around the world. But most normal people didn't ever see it. If I told you the name you wouldn't know it. And that's why, as brilliant a filmmaker as he is, he's a film professor and not a super wealthy director. Now, you know who else studied at my film school? Danny Allen. Ever hear of him?"

"Yes. Everyone know Danny Allen."

"Exactly. Because he made *Only the Brave*, which every person on earth saw. And *Omega Brigade*. And *Love and War*. And the list goes on. And he made a ton of money. And he didn't become a film school professor. He has millions and millions of dollars because all of his movies sell a shitload of tickets." In service to the point I was trying to make, I left out my feelings on how formulaic and lame I actually found his films to be. "Do you follow me?"

"Follow you?"

"Do you understand what I'm saying so far?"

"All but not where to follow you," Purwoko said.

"Yes. All. But follow you where?" Gita asked in solidarity.

"Let's forget the follow part. The tickets that Danny Allen sells are like the product your client wants to sell. Don't worry about winning the awards but not selling the tickets. Sell the tickets. If you want more money, you make the work that sells. That's the work that makes more money. And if you do that with me I will promise to get you more money. Okay?"

"So, we only do work for clients want now?"

"Exactly."

"But clients only want the bad work."

"So give it to them. Trust me. If you want to make money, give the clients what they want. And if you want to make tons of money, give the clients what they want but in a way that sells a lot of their product as well."

"But we want to do the good work to win the award."

"And you also want more money?"

"Yes," they both said in unison.

"Please, just follow my lead for now. I really want to help you. I made a lot of money in my career by listening to the client and . . ." Just as I was building momentum in what I thought would be a life-changing motivational speech for these men, the calls to prayer bellowed through the city, through my window, into my office. Purwoko and Gita stood.

"We go pray now, Mr. Paul." They walked out. I turned to see my friend in the village pouring water from one pot to another, oblivious to the prayers. Oblivious to his friend, the voyeur, in the window above the moat. But I now had the information I needed. I knew our common ground. As he went about his business, allowing the holy frequencies to slither past him like the angel of death around a doorframe brushed with lamb's blood, I saw then that we were both men beyond the influence of any god.

CHAPTER 11

"Paul, I found you a wonderful house," Nisa said one morning.

"What for?" I asked.

"You can't keep living in a hotel. You'll never feel like you belong here."

"That's a good reason. Where is this house?"

"Very close. In Kemang. Many foreigners like to live there."

"But I don't want to live where foreigners live. I should be among the people."

"Like in the Four Seasons?"

"Fair enough. But if I'm going to the trouble to plant roots . . ."

"Kemang also has many Indonesians. Don't worry. It is a good mix for you. And a beautiful house. It is the former house of my former boss."

"Another creative director?" I asked.

"Yes. Does that matter?"

"Was he better than I am?"

"He was not as young as you are."

"Interesting."

"Also, maybe not as funny."

I thought about it and decided that it would be nice to have a house in town. To feel like a resident instead of a tourist. "When can I see it?"

"I will tell Rahim to get the car now."

If I had to describe the house in one word, I'd call it "cavernous." The main entrance opened to a grand room in which I could have fit a Roller Derby rink. In the far corner of the room, there was a full-size, four-person sofa, a coffee table, and a large, old, vacuum-tube television on a brass stand that was bulging from the weight. In my last New York City apartment the furniture would have packed the living room. Here, in relation to the space, the furniture seemed built for a dollhouse. I couldn't imagine what it would take to furnish the room so that it felt properly lived in. But the reason none of that mattered, and what instantly closed the deal for me, was the wall of large glass doors opening up to a colonial-style back porch sitting over a quaint, tropical garden. I didn't need to see anything else. If every other room were infested with rodents, I would have set up a hammock and lived back there in the garden.

As I stepped out past the porch into the well-manicured Eden, I found to my right a small pool with a stone patio around it. I could see it in a Bertolucci film: a couple of young students on summer break, casually fornicating on a centuries-old lawn blanket while an alluring, middle-age woman sat in the shade, sketching in her journal, and a fat, bearded, elderly man swam slow and steady laps. There was a rustic wooden recliner, perfectly warped, in which I imagined many pages of prose would be written. Cement walls in charming distress lined the far side of the pool, and geckos chased each other across the cracks. I turned to Nisa. "I'll take it."

"That's great, Paul. They said you can spend a few nights here and make sure you like it," she replied.

"I can move in today?" I asked with excitement.

"Yes, Paul. They left the couch and television behind, so those are all yours if you'd like them. Also there is a bed in the master bedroom."

"This is all perfect, Nisa. Thank you."

"Just one more thing," she added. "The last tenant had a house staff. A maid, Tetti. She can cook and clean and take care of any shopping for you. Also, there is a pool boy and also a gardener, who is the husband of Tetti. Would you like to keep them all as staff?"

"I feel like I'd be crazy not to."

"I was hoping you'd say that. I'll arrange everything."

I walked back inside and saw Rahim looking around, inspecting corners. "What do you think, Rahim?" I asked.

"Hmm. Very big for only one. Maybe you live here you need the family," he said.

Nisa laughed to herself.

"Don't laugh at Rahim, Nisa. Maybe I'll find a family to live here with me."

"As in, tenants?"

We both laughed then. Rahim smiled. "I think the family will be good, Paul. Very good for you."

"Hey! Nisa! I just had an amazing idea!" I blurted out.

"Paul," she replied in a motherly tone, "please at least wait until a lease agreement is signed before you ask me if the poor man from the village can live here with you."

Now Rahim laughed, and the two of us walked out to the car while Nisa settled things in the house.

"I think the man of village very lucky if he live with you, Paul. With you and the family. Very lucky. Very good for everyone," Rahim said to me when we got in the car.

"Thank you, Rahim. That's very sweet of you to say. I think so too. I'm going to tell Nisa you said that."

"Please, no. She kill me," he said with a grin.

Later, when Rahim dropped us off at the office, Nisa instructed him to collect my things from the hotel and take them to the house so they'd be there for me when I returned.

I was so excited about the Goldberg Estate, as I began calling it, that the rest of the day was a blur. Some meetings. Some more meetings. My friend in the village poured some sort of dark liquid into half a dozen liter-size plastic bottles. I imagined coming home to toast my friend and new roommate as his mystery liquid worked its way cancerously through my digestive track.

I did manage to distract myself from daydreams long

enough to help some teams improve various commercial scripts. They all questioned me when I told them to mention the product at least once more or to strengthen the visualization of a benefit. I tried my best to explain my feedback and direction, and they mostly smiled at me, which seemed to be as much as I could ask for.

Toward the end of the day I walked out of the bathroom to find Santi scolding one of my creative staff and him yelling back at her. I couldn't understand a word of it but felt it my responsibility to intervene.

"What's going on, team?" I asked in a positive tone, hoping to diffuse the tension.

"Mr. Paul. I know you want to do what the client wants, but I think they are wrong here. I think they can sell more this new way. Not just for award. For better work, Mr. Paul. To sell more the product, like you say," Eric said.

"But it's too late now," Santi explained. "We are too late. And they have said what they want. It is very clear already, you see."

Normally, I'd have taken her side. But I did want my staff to feel like I was in it with them. If I disagreed with them, I wanted to keep it behind closed doors. I needed them to feel like I had their backs. And in this particular case, I was especially curious. Something about Eric's passion struck me. It made me want to help him all the more. The fact that he was differentiating between a better idea for the sake of awards and a better idea that would actually be good for the client piqued my interest. As he explained the idea, I instantly saw where he was going with it.

"Hey, Santi," I interrupted, "let's give him a couple of days to figure it out. I agree that it might be in the client's interest."

"But they need ideas today, Paul. You know this client," she said.

"I do. And I understand your position. But do me a favor and push them off for a day or two while Eric works on this. I'll help him."

"But, cannot," she said.

"Come on. Just give it a shot. What do we have to lose?"

"We can lose the client."

"We won't lose the fucking client, Santi," I said. She looked at me with surprise. I'd never pushed back like that before, but I knew that Eric was right. "Just tell them we're working on something special for them and that they won't be disappointed."

I extended a hand for a high five. Santi stormed away, leaving me hanging. I cocked my head like a dog awaiting an explanation.

"Thank you, Mr. Paul!" Eric was overjoyed. "You will help me make new idea good for client? Maybe good for the client and for the award but not the scam, right?"

"I think there's a lot of potential in it. Why don't you spend the evening thinking about how to make it work, and then in the morning we'll go over it together. Just remember, for a great idea to work, it needs to lead to a consumer action. Let's aim for an award-winning idea that a client will be excited to buy because the consumer will actually feel great about their product after seeing it."

"Okay, Mr. Paul," Eric said. "You are right maybe."

"I like to think so."

"But I think maybe you should not have said, 'the fuck' with Santi."

"Really? I'm sure she's heard worse."

"Maybe her husband believe it offensive?"

"Well how the fuck will her husband know?"

"Indonesia, Mr. Paul." He gave me a serious look to make sure I understood he wasn't talking about domestic traffic patterns.

"She'll be fine. I think the context was reasonable."

"Inshallah."

"Indeed."

CHAPTER 12

"Hey Paul Jewberg. How is Jakarta for you. Enjoy now. Your days soon will end."

I raised a victorious fist in the air, knowing immediately that this text message would make for a great shift in the momentum of my story. Then I wondered how seriously I should take the threat. I knew that strange and dangerous things happened in this part of the world. It wasn't unheard of for people to disappear in corners of the earth such as this one. But I couldn't imagine anyone I might have wronged to this extent. I hadn't slept with any married women. At least, I didn't think so. Of course, looking back, it should have been more obvious. It was only a day after Eric told me I shouldn't have said "the fuck" with Santi. But would anyone in my shoes have thought of that then?

I didn't want to come off as worried, male pride and all. Nor did I want to fail to take a serious threat to heart. I replied in a manner that I thought worthy of a man from Stonetown, a man who had been specifically instructed to "represent."

"Who the fuck is this?" I tapped into my phone and

hit send. Then I waited to see what would happen. I didn't have to wait long.

"Who I am not important. Your worst nightmare for sure. I sharpen my knife now. What is your favorite body part? I guess what to take first."

Vacillating between alarm and wonder, I naively tried to guess from whom this could be. I looked out my office window and saw my friend hunched beside a shed of some sort, digging through a wooden trunk. I wondered if he was capable of these texts. How funny it would've been if, the entire time I thought I was observing him, he was the one observing me, doing his research. Finding out who is that man in the window? What sorts of evil does he bring with him to our country? What Western propaganda does this man spread? Through what capitalist nonsense does he corrupt the nation's youth? By what means does he infect our culture with his atheist beliefs? This Paul Goldberg. This Jew by birth. This enemy of Indonesia.

I decided I should reply to the text and then watch my friend. Watch to see if he'd reach for a phone. Watch for any reaction, any show of emotion at all.

"My favorite body part? My fist when it breaks through your teeth. So, who is this?"

The boys in Stonetown would have enjoyed that one. They'd also have been more than prepared to back it up. I smiled and imagined fighting alongside them in a brawl. Then I wished that I had joined them at least once, to know what it was like. My clenched fist ached to know the reverberations of bones when they make impact with a face. I anticipated the adrenaline rush that would follow the sound of a jaw dislocating at my behest. If I could have just once experienced a real fight, it might have readied me for this situation. I wondered if fighting wasn't as bad as I had always imagined. If the losers didn't feel as much pain as they always did in my mind. If the winners earned a rite of passage I hadn't considered. Was this the true way? Were we pacifists the ones frustrating human nature and progress, going against the master plan of the greater animal world where violence plays an integral and undeniable role? Was that god's will?

Days went by, and the texts went back and forth. I'd receive a text. I'd send a text. I'd watch from the window, and I'd never see my friend react after one of my texts. I never saw him with a phone at all. He appeared innocent. My friend, still.

I went with Eric to help present his idea to the bank client, though I let him run the presentation. He said all the right things, hit all the right strategic points, and the work was well received. The client committed on the spot to put a fair budget behind it. Santi, in private, begrudgingly admitted that it was a good thing I had postponed the meeting to help Eric perfect his idea.

The creative department responded positively to the news and began to see me as an ally finally. They came to me for help. They wanted to know how to make their ideas better, more sellable. In turn, I had a newfound desire to help them dream up ideas that were worthy of awards. Help them find the balance. Find it with them. I wanted them to be proud of what we were all working toward. I helped them push for better, and I pushed with them. With clients like Indra, I had earned trust through increased sales, and he especially was more open to taking my word for what path would be best. Over the course of several months, we had created some great work. Work that would sell products and possibly win awards as well. With all of the resources at my disposal in New York, I had never thought such a balance was possible. Yet here I was in the Third World, a ragtag team of passionate creatives in my charge, learning what was possible, what might have been possible all along.

"I'm happy when I see you bonding with the staff more and more," Nisa said one day as we ate lunch on the couch in my office.

"They've been good. They're working hard."

"Yes, they are working hard. But they have lives. What about you?"

"Life? Well, it's been okay. I go out a lot."

"With your friends Justin and Jeff?"

"Yup."

"And when do you get to know the Indonesians you wanted so badly to be amongst?"

"Well, I've gotten to know some."

"Other than the women you . . ."

"Philippe has a local wife," I interrupted. "I've been to their home and met their local friends."

"And will you ever have a local wife?"

"I don't know, Nisa. Things are just getting started. Things are good now. I haven't even gotten a death-threat text in a few days."

"A what kind of text?"

I was sorry I'd mentioned it. "Nothing."

"Paul. What is it?" she pushed.

"I didn't want to worry you, but I have been getting text messages from someone saying they were going to cut my body parts off and kill me and whatnot."

"And whatnot?"

I showed her the text history, and her face alternated between horror and amusement. "Paul, you shouldn't have said these things. But some of them are very funny." She looked at me with concern. "You'll rip off his head and shit into his neck? Paul! What kind of thing is this to say?"

"I heard a friend say it before getting into a fight once. I thought it was a good one. Kind of threatening, no?"

"Not as threatening as what he said in return."

"Don't worry. It's over now. He hasn't replied in a while."

"What about this morning?"

"Huh?"

"They know where you live?"

She showed me the phone, and there was one text I hadn't read. I must have scrolled past it, through the dozens of work messages I usually wake up to.

"I hope you have no plans this night. You and my knife will meet for final. 11 Kemang Ria, see you soon."

"Okay, that one might be slightly concerning," I offered.

"Paul, I don't like this. Maybe you should stay somewhere else tonight."

"Really?"

"I think so. Maybe a hotel. Or . . . if you need there is room at my home."

"Nisa, that's sweet, but I couldn't. I'll get a hotel. If it makes you feel better. It's no problem. Or I can always stay with my friend in the village next door."

She laughed, and I promised her I'd go to a hotel that night. I asked her to call my house staff and tell them to take the rest of the day off. I doubted anything would happen, but I thought it best to keep them safe.

I woke up with a considerable hangover the next morning. Petra was lying next to me, watching me sleep. We had been on a few dates since our first enlightening night together, and I felt there was potential for us to become exclusive soon.

"I spoke to my parents," she said when it seemed I was awake enough to comprehend words.

"What about?"

"About you."

"Oh? What about me?"

"I told them you are the Jew. But they don't mind."

"How worldly of them. But I told you I don't believe in religion. I was only born that way."

"But you're not Muslim."

"That's correct."

"They said that even if you are not Muslim. And if you are not the Jew but your family is the Jew. Even though our people really don't like the Jew, but if I love you and you are the good man, they say it is okay for us to marry."

I sat up. "Marry?"

"Yes. Is it wonderful?"

I smiled cautiously while trying to phrase my thoughts delicately. "I'm happy that they accept me. A non-Muslim and all of that. It sounds like a very promising road toward world peace. But we've only been together less than a handful of times. You're great. I'm not ready to marry you though."

"But I want to marry you."

"I'd like to date you more. Can we date? Like girlfriend and boyfriend?"

"When will we marry if we date?"

"I don't know. If we date for a year or two and fall in love, then I would consider it." It was the best I could offer, and it seemed like a safe gamble.

"A year? I can't wait a year. I want to get married soon. When I go to weddings I am very sad that I am not married yet."

"I hate to say this, but I'm not the one who is going to marry you right now. I'd like to date you. I mean it."

"I can't. I want to marry. I'm sorry."

"I'm sorry too." I hugged her and felt something for her but not love. Respect, maybe. Pity, mostly. The anticipation of missing the sex with her and her preternatural vaginal abilities, definitely. My phone rang, and I didn't want to answer it, but I saw that it was Nisa calling so I answered.

"Where are you, Paul?" She was frantic.

"Calm down, Nisa. I'm at the Four Seasons. Like I promised. And a little hungover. So, please don't yell."

"Paul, I was trying to call all morning. Your home . . ."

"What?"

"Everything is gone. Tetti called. Someone broke into your home. They took everything."

CHAPTER 13

I arrived at the house by motorbike taxi to find an entirety of neighborhood kids in my driveway. My maid, Tetti, and my gardener, her husband, Ali, were there looking worried. I think they felt guilty, and I walked over to hug Tetti, hoping to reassure them all. Ali gave me a strange glance, and I wasn't sure that my hug translated the way I'd hoped.

I felt a hand on my shoulder and turned to find Rahim, who must have arrived just after I had. He looked at me with gentle, sympathetic eyes. I wanted to hug him too. I shook his hand.

"The policeman say he ready to search house, you want," he said.

"The police haven't gone in yet?"

"No. Only Tetti. But she run out when she see they break door. Not know if still inside. Bad men."

"Oh? These guys might still be inside?"

"Maybe. Police want you go in with him."

"Okay. I'll do it. Wanna come too?"

"I come too," Rahim answered as if there were nothing else in the world he'd choose to do at that moment.

I greeted the officer with a handshake without realizing he was holding a revolver in his right hand. He switched the gun to his left hand and gave me a weak handshake that inspired little confidence in me. We entered the house through the garage, which led directly into the kitchen, and I felt Rahim's presence behind me. But then I turned and looked and saw every kid in the neighborhood was behind him. Maybe ten to twelve of them varying in age from four or five to young teens. Anchoring the line behind the children was a mysterious man who I would later learn was the neighbor's security guard. I wished I had known to have one myself. I had the requisite maid, gardener, and pool boy that my position in local society required. But I had neglected the security guard. Hell, I could have given the pool boy some extra rupiah to guard the house. Surely he could have been at least as intimidating as the man peeking over a young girl's pigtails. I told myself I would deal with it later.

The kitchen appeared untouched, although, admittedly, there really wasn't very much to touch. I had bought some luxury chef's knives for Tetti to use, but she liked them so much she asked permission to take them home every night to cook her family dinner. I never had a problem with that, and it turned out to be a good way to keep the knives safe.

The officer checked my fridge and examined the lone bowl of fresh fruit found inside. Tetti must have cut it up for me the day prior. I took it and handed it to one of the kids behind Rahim, hoping he'd share it with the others. He didn't. I could hear him slurping his way through it as he walked behind me.

My couch was still lounging away in the living room, in the same corner of that vast, empty space. The TV was not, but that's because I had given it to the house staff. There wasn't always very much for them to do during the day so I worried they'd be bored and so moved it to their rest area above the garage. I turned and whispered to Rahim, "Is the TV still there?"

"If no, Tetti kill bad guy," he said. We both let out a soft giggle and turned back to the task at hand. We were about to enter the first of the five bedrooms. The officer peered in the room, turned on the light, and turned toward us with his revolver in locked pivot with his line of sight. I ducked out of the way.

"They take everything!" he exclaimed in a whisper, finally pointing his gun downward.

"Oh. Actually, there wasn't anything in that bedroom," I assured him. He looked at me quizzically, and Rahim explained it to him in Bahasa. Then the officer gave me a new quizzical look, and I imagined this time it was for different reasons. He went deeper into the room, I assumed to check for perpetrators hiding in a closet. I waited in the hallway, but the kids followed him in. Moments later he emerged satisfied, the stragglers close behind. Two of the children now held wire hangers, which they had shaped into swordlike forms. We repeated this formality with the other three empty bedrooms before arriving at my actual bedroom. By this time all of the children were armed with makeshift weaponry. One boy had half of a broken closet beam and the pigtail girl had the other half of it. Before the officer entered my bedroom, Rahim explained to him that this was the room that actually should have things in it. The officer opened the door, revolver first, peeked inside, and let out a groan. He told the children something in Bahasa and walked in alone. A few seconds later he waved me in with his revolver hand and I entered, no longer bothering to duck out of the way of the gun barrel.

In my room, every drawer had been ripped out of place. The bed was flipped over and the sheets ripped off, an unnecessarily rude act, I felt. Clothes hangers were scattered, lacking their designated clothes. One of the kids traded his hanger for one he must have considered to be better. Everything in the room was in a place other than where it belonged. But I knew instantly what wasn't there. Computer. Camera. Hard drive. A custom-made hunting knife from a little bespoke shop in Tennessee. Dress shoes. An emergency wad of cash. The clothes, I guessed, were taken just as a "fuck you." Though they were very nice clothes. Whoever the hell it was had also gone ahead and taken my luggage, probably to make it easier for themselves to drag my belongings out of my home. But again, it was very nice luggage.

Some of the pilfered items, like the camera and computer and clothing, were expensive, sure. The money was money. And some other particulars were of ranging levels of sentimental value. But nothing hurt worse than the hard drive. On it was everything I'd ever written. Brilliant, stupid, honest ideas that would never see the light of day. There were short stories I'd hoped to publish as a collection after I had become a successful novelist. Short film sketches I'd been playing with. A screenplay for a feature-length, less artsy, more commercially viable follow-up to my *Seventeen* short. Every thought, every phrase, every outline that would one day become an amazing something. Also missing was a thick folder containing every poem I'd ever written in my life. Each a one-of-a-kind original. I looked around for that, hoping it might be under the mess, thinking it was the one thing of value to me they might have left, having no practical value to them. Then I remembered that I kept it in the laptop sleeve of my carry-on, and what little wind was left in me fled the scene. I'd always dreamed I'd destroy my poems one day in a drug-induced fit of rage after a passionate quarrel with a yet-to-be-determined soul mate. The coldhearted bandits had taken that imagined scenario from me as well.

One boy collected all of the coins from off the floor and handed the pile to me, as if it might help. I thanked him with a smile and handed it back to him, hoping he'd share it with the other kids. He didn't. The money that did matter was a stack of US currency valuing ten thousand dollars. Ironically, I'd withdrawn it and kept it in said carry-on as part of a go kit on Jeff's recommendation when I'd first mentioned the threats to him. In his defense, he'd also told me to keep that go kit in the car or hidden in my office.

Eventually, the officer ushered everyone back out to the front yard, where several other policemen were casually smoking cigarettes. I sat on a large ornamental lawn rock while Rahim spoke with them. There were people walking in and out, and by the time Rahim explained to me that they were dusting for prints, I'd already accepted the fact that I wouldn't be seeing my things again.

I looked at the text messages again and thought to do the one thing I hadn't done, which should have been my first thought after the first text. I called the number.

"Hello, Bule," he answered on the first ring.

"I'm glad you answered." I was. "What have you done, man? And what have I done to deserve this?" I was trying to keep my cool.

"You shouldn't mess with the local girl, Bule."

"What local girl did I mess with?"

"You say 'the fuck' with my wife, fucking Bule. Now you pay."

"The fuck? What?"

"You say 'the fuck' with my wife. You disrespect my wife. Santi."

"Holy shit! Really? That's what this is about? I used

a curse word in front of Santi? I curse in front of everyone, man."

"Yes. I am the husband of Santi. And soon you will regret everything in your life. You should not say 'the fuck' with the local girl, fucking Jew Bule."

"Fucking hell, I'm an atheist. I mean, I remember what you're talking about. I did say that word, but I didn't mean what I think you think I meant by it. Santi and I are friendly. I didn't mean it in a bad way."

"There is no other way. You say 'the fuck.' You disrespect my wife. Now I disrespect you."

"Well, don't you think you've done enough?"

"Not enough until it is finished."

"And how exactly does it get finished?" I had a feeling but now wanted to hear it come out of his mouth.

"You apologize to Santi or die by my knife."

"Fuck you!" It left my mouth without warning.

"Bule. You will apologize to Santi, or you will die soon."

"How about I just hand my phone to the police who are at my house?"

"Give them phone, and I have them arrest you." I was skeptical but something in me believed this to be a possibility. I said "Fuck you" once more for good measure and hung up.

Unsettled and slightly panicked from it all, I called Nisa, who explained to me that Santi's husband was the son of a very well-known general. He was also his father's right hand and reputed to sometimes carry out certain acts of political retribution at his father's request.

"Paul," Nisa said, "you need to apologize."

"That's not going to happen."

"Paul. Please don't be crazy. He can kill you and get away with it. Please, apologize as he says."

I told her I needed some time to think, and when we hung up I found Rahim and asked him to drive me to Jeff's house.

"Dude! What's up? No work today?" Jeff asked when he opened his front door and I walked right in.

"Man, I really need a drink."

"I was just about to go for a swim but, yeah, a drink works too."

Sitting in a lounge chair on Jeff's back patio, I filled him in on what had transpired. We tried to laugh about as much as there was to laugh about, both knowing it wasn't a laughing matter.

"On a serious note though, you need to call the embassy," he suggested.

"The embassy? Which one?"

"Ha! Yours. Ours, man."

"So they can call in the secretary of state and negotiate a peace treaty?"

"Dude, I'm serious," he said. "You call the fucking embassy. You tell them to get some marines over to this guy's house and break his fucking teeth in. Kick his ass.

Tell him not to fuck with Americans here. You know how much shit our country is letting this place get away with? The amounts of corruption to which our government turns its cheek just to keep things simple for the oil guys? Man, you can ask your boy Scotty about that."

"Let's leave that guy out of this."

"Fair enough. But I mean it. These dudes don't want to piss off the Americans, no matter who this guy is. He's not gonna do shit if a bunch of marines show up to his house with brass knuckles."

"I love the sound of all this, but is that even an option?"

"I may have gotten a little bit excited with the brass knuckles. But fuck yeah. Who do you think really runs this joint?"

"The corrupt Indonesian military. One of the heads of which is the father of the dude who had my house trashed and wants to kill me."

"Young grasshopper, there's always someone more important, someone with more money and more guns. And that's the American presence here. They allow that shit to exist out of the goodness of their hearts and the hunger of their wallets. Call the fucking embassy."

"Okay. Can we drink some more beers first? I need to chill out for a minute."

"Fuck yeah. Drink as much as you'd like. I can break out the good shit too if you want."

"I like that plan."

"Right on."

I drank my beer and stared at the pool beyond my pasty white toes. Simon and Garfunkel were on Jeff's music mix. I smiled, thinking of the scene from *The Graduate* when Dustin Hoffman is in the pool. Back in film school I was obsessed with that movie in general and that scene specifically. There's no great reason, really. Cinematically it's quite simple, but there's always been something poetic about it. Then, as if working in partnership with some governing body of the solar system to say to me "You want to see poetic, motherfucker?," the Dead's "Brokedown Palace" came on. In the next chapter I'll explain why that's significant. And why I made the decision I was about to make.

CHAPTER 14

On the Sunday morning after college graduation, my friend Gary, while driving home from the infamous 6:00 a.m. happy hour at our favorite bar, the River, was obliterated by a sixteen-wheeler. Gary was driving the wrong way in the wrong lane. I like to imagine he was too drunk to have known what was happening. Experiencing an event like that with full awareness just seems too far beyond tragic to me.

His family offered to fly a small group of friends to his funeral in Northern California. Everyone went except for Pedro and me, though we were his best friends. Our mutual opinion at the time was that there was nothing to be done at a funeral. There were better ways to honor Gary's life and our memories of him.

We procured a large bag of mushrooms, a boom box, and two In-N-Out burgers, animal style, on which we placed the divided caps and stems. When we found ourselves far enough into an area outside of Palm Springs that most resembled what we imagined the middle of nowhere to be like, and I could bear the responsibility of the wheel no longer, I pulled over. The landscape was hot, unforgiving, brutal. The perfect place for our spiritual flagellation.

I confessed to Pedro that I had seen Gary just before he went off to that 6:00 a.m. happy hour. He was looking for a partner in crime, and as tempting as 6:00 a.m. happy hour had always been, I was too busy flirting with a girl who was way out of my league but deceivingly friendly. I wasn't sure how guilty to feel about that, if at all.

"It doesn't matter, man," Pedro assured me. "It's not like you wish you'd gone with him. That's not you. And that's not your story. So don't worry about it for a second. If you hadn't been fooling yourself into thinking you'd get that chick, you either would have gone with him or not, and either way you never in a million years would have talked him out of going. Let's just let it be and honor his life by pressing play on this tape."

He pulled a cassette tape out of his pocket and commanded my attention toward the label, on which was written "For Gary—A Legendary Mixtape."

"You made a mixtape for the occasion? I love it."

"Paul. You're never going to believe me. But believe me when I say I'm aware of the irony or the hypocrisy or whatever about all of what I just said . . . but I'm also tripping my face off on a lot of mushrooms, so please stick with me on it."

"Okay. What? Just say it, dude!"

"I made this tape for him on Sunday morning."

"But you were with me when we found out Sunday afternoon."

"That's what I'm saying. The night before, he was like, 'Yo, Pedro. For my graduation gift I want one of your legendary mixtapes.' So, I was all coked up and couldn't fall asleep, and I spent the morning making this mix for him."

"You were making his mix while he was dying?"

"It's some heavy shit right there, no?"

"It is some heavy shit right there. Please, just put that tape in right now."

The average man might have opened a mixtape labeled as "legendary" with a song that had some umph to it. Something that really opened things up with high energy. But Pedro was never an average man, and so he had opened the mix with Gary's favorite song, "Brokedown Palace." Which also happened to be the song that was playing when the three of us became friends.

I was walking through the hallway of my freshman year dormitory when I heard the song playing from one of the rooms. I stuck my head in and mentioned how much I loved the Grateful Dead and what a great song it was. Gary invited me in to take a hit from his bong. Then, before I was able to close the door behind me, someone else popped their head in the door and started singing along with the song, word for word. Gary and I looked at each other with deep understanding and wide grins. Then Gary invited Pedro in, and said, "Close the door. Take a hit from my bong. I also have methamphetamines if anyone's into it."

In the years that followed, the three of us were as tight as could be.

"It's too brutal. But so great," I said to Pedro.

"I know."

"I feel like I'm being punched in the stomach by an elephant."

"I know."

"Do me a favor?"

"Yup."

"Rewind it to the beginning of the song. I want to lie back and listen to the whole thing without talking. With my eyes closed. I want to see if I can drown my heart with tears."

"You got it, buddy."

Within weeks of our desert memorial service, Pedro moved to Austin, Texas. We promised that, no matter where we lived, we'd meet somewhere in the country once a year and take a long drive with that mixtape each time. The first year we met in Boise and drove to Ketchum, to Hemingway's grave. The next year we met in Seattle and visited the graves of Jimi Hendrix and Bruce Lee.

For the third year we had plans to visit a birthplace instead of a grave site, but before we could settle on an idea, Pedro died in a plane crash. It was one of those single engine prop jobs. The kind that rock stars die in. So, I ended up going to another grave that year after all. His family was never able to find that mixtape for me.

CHAPTER 15

My musically induced flashback was interrupted by the cold nudge of a glass of Pappy Van Winkle, on the rocks, against my shoulder. I took a slow sip to the core of my being. It tasted like the last drink of a disgraced dictator, just before his public execution.

"If you need me to tell you what that is, you don't deserve it. But it's the twenty-three-year."

"I do deserve it. Right now, I do," I said. "I'm going to apologize, by the way."

"What?"

"To Santi. And her husband. Mostly to her. You know the deal here. They're all about saving face. If I push him he can't back down. If I apologize he wins. He saves face. I live to write about it. You may be right that it's not in their interest to kill an American. But I don't think it's completely out of the question."

Hendrix was singing to me through the stereo now, and I was holding back tears. I felt the presence of ghosts I wasn't prepared to join. I felt them pushing me on, wanting me to continue the journey for them. Jeff sipped his drink with pride and marinated on what

I had said. "Here Comes the Sun" by the Beatles came and went before Radiohead's "Karma Police" played and Jeff spoke.

"It could work," he offered, standing up and moseying toward the pool.

"Really?"

"Yeah. You should do it. Tomorrow. Not today."

"Okay."

"You're right about the other part too."

"Which part is that?" I asked.

"You'll live to write about it. Put it in your book. And quote me. In fact, write that I said what I just said while putting my glass down like this, just before diving in, and how it looked all cool and shit."

As Jeff said that, he placed his empty rocks glass on the rear edge of the diving board and executed a swan dive with perfect form and almost no splash.

When I knocked on the door of Santi's office the next day, I had a knot in my throat and an oversize, button-down shirt that I had borrowed from Jeff on my back. She invited me in with a cold welcome. I apologized for using the f-word with her and reiterated that it didn't mean what she thought it meant, but that I was sorry anyway. I should have been more culturally aware and had more respect for local norms and sensitivities, I explained. She, in return, and to her credit, apologized to me on behalf of her husband, "for the death threats and all of those things." She didn't acknowledge the break-in, and I wasn't sure if it mattered at that point.

What really launched my brains right out of my skull, though, was when, after a brief moment of post-apology, awkward silence, she asked if I was dating anyone in Jakarta.

"Are you serious?" I asked.

"Serious? Of course I am serious. I have very beautiful single friends. And my cousin is single as well. Very sexy girl."

"Can I think about it?" I didn't know what else to say. Saying "the fuck" came to mind, but I kept it to myself.

"Have it your way. You know where to find me when you decide. Now I better get back to work. Busy busy." She smiled at me and turned to her computer and started typing. I imagined that she was writing something about expanding the reach of product sampling in rural areas throughout the Indonesian islands.

I left her office, and instead of going to mine, I walked straight out to the parking lot to see if Rahim was still around. I found him hustling the other drivers in some card game I'd never seen before. As soon as he saw me he dropped his cards and ran over.

"Hey Rahim. Sorry to interrupt. I know you weren't expecting me yet."

"Is no problem, Paul. I win more later." He gave me a smile that was sort of like a wink. I laughed and put my hand on his shoulder.

"Tell me, my man. How far a drive is it to Bali?"

"Drive Bali? You go the meeting? Why no fly?"

"No meeting. I just need a break and thought it'd be more dramatic to drive."

"Oh. Hmm. But very far the drive. Maybe one day. But traffic also. Indonesia. Maybe two day?"

"Right. It may take a full day just to leave Jakarta. Just drop me at the airport."

"Okay, Paul. What time?"

"Now would be great."

"You fly Bali now? We go your home first. Your bags?"

"I don't have luggage anymore, remember?"

"Oh. Yes. Sorry, Paul."

"It's okay. I'll purchase some sort of indigenous attire when I land. Maybe even a bag to keep it all in."

"What?"

"Don't worry about it. Let's go to the airport."

"Yes, Paul. I think you like Bali. Maybe rest for some day. Relax. Then back Jakarta. Everything good."

CHAPTER 16

I didn't know the truth about Lusi until after I had already fallen in love with her. We were at Sky Club in Bali, and when I first saw her standing at the edge of the dance floor, her smile bright and inviting, her eyes like twin planets, our gazes locked. She guided me in, the narrowing of her eyelids acting like a tractor beam. Time slowed. The journey toward her felt like a pilgrimage to my own personal holy land. After what seemed to be forty years in the desert I found myself standing face to face with her, thinking to avert my eyes from hers, unable to focus on anything else. I'm a moderate and often cynical romantic, but it wouldn't be out of line for me to say that this was love at first sight.

"Hi," was all I could get out in a breath.

"Hi," she replied. "I see you look. I wait you."

"Thank you for waiting. I'm Paul."

"Paul. Is nice name. I Lusi."

"Hi Lusi. Are you here with friends?"

"No."

"Can I buy you a drink?" I asked, hoping to extend the interaction for as close to forever as possible.

"Juice is okay?"

"Anything you want is fine. You wouldn't prefer beer or wine or anything else?"

"I no drink alcohol because I Muslim," she said.

If my brain were working properly, this might have signaled a red flag. Of the women I had been with since arriving in Indonesia, all of them drank despite their religion. I might have guessed that a Muslim girl strict enough not to drink would also be unwilling to become involved with the infidel. But none of that processed in my brain at the time. I didn't consider how strict her religious beliefs might have been. I didn't care what she drank. And I wasn't interested in the hundred or so other attractive, booze-fueled women dancing around us to the thumping tones of David Guetta. I only cared about getting Lusi her juice and keeping her by my side for as long as my heart continued to pump blood through my veins.

Leaning against the bar with ease, she sipped her drink through a pink cocktail straw while I told her about my time in Jakarta. Her questions were simple but sincere. They included the standard checklist of where I was from, if I was married, if I had a girlfriend, and if I was lying. Then, disarming me, she asked, "What dream you have?" Unsure of whether she meant ambitions or the dreams that come during sleep, I answered, "The scary kind." She laughed. I melted.

"Funny man. Not this dream like in the sleep. What you dream for? For you life. In English is same?"

"Ah, yes. Of course. I'm sorry. I wasn't sure what dreams you meant, but I understand now."

"Good. So, what?"

"I don't know, actually."

"You no want for nothing? No dream?"

"Well, it's not that. It's just that when I was younger I had all sorts of dreams. I wanted to be a writer. And then I wanted to make movies because it was like poetry of all the senses. And then I decide that I wanted to make a lot of money. And then I wanted to make more money. And then I realized that I had forgotten about all my real dreams. I felt so uninteresting that I wanted to come here to live a more interesting life and gather enough material to write a book. And then shit kind of hit the fan and my life in Jakarta fell apart and I came here to Bali to reevaluate everything. My hope is that by the time I leave here I'll have new dreams and a new focus and perhaps even some newfound motivation. Maybe you'll be a part of my new dream." At this last part, she laughed. I wasn't sure if it was a laugh at me or with me, but I enjoyed her laugh so much. It was guttural and unladylike. It was no beauty queen laugh. It was downright nerdy, and I adored it.

"Heh heh heh. You marry me?" Lusi asked, her smile illuminating the room.

"Well, maybe after I get to know you. But. Maybe. Why not?"

"Okay. Maybe. But I think now I go. We talk very

much, long time. Don't want my customer watch." She squeezed one of my fingers, quickly withdrew her hand, and looked around conspiratorially.

"Oh, you work here? I didn't even realize." Of course, I thought, an establishment like this would hire her as a hostess. She'd keep people coming back from miles away. "You're the hostess?"

"No. I *working* here," she stressed with widened eyes.

"Yeah, I get that. But what do you do? Manager?"

She laughed. "No, I *working* here. You know?" She gave me a look, a plea for me not to make her say it aloud. But my naivete failed us both. I shrugged.

"I working girl. *Working* here." Finally, she leaned closer and said in a softer tone, almost a whisper, "I prostitute."

It's difficult to tell what thoughts my face might have betrayed when she said it. I tried to play it cool, surprised though I was. I had nothing against prostitutes, per se. I'd even received a blow job from one once. It was at the wrap party for *To me, This Is 17*. I was bummed out about having been rejected by several girls in a row at the party, despite being the creator of the film we were celebrating. Benji, Compton crack dealer, friend, and newly minted film producer, gave me a pep talk and introduced me to one of his girls, Sin. Benji said that if I took Sin to the back room with an eighth of crack she'd give me the best blow job I'd ever had. I didn't take a statement like this, coming from a man of his station, lightly. During the summer after high school graduation

I'd read *Pimp* by Iceberg Slim, and I'd had one particular scene impressed upon my memory ever since.

Ice and another pimp were posturing about whose whores had the better skills, and Ice presented one of his ladies as the most talented fellatio artist ever to walk the earth. To which the rival pimp retorted that no bitch born to man could make him ejaculate by way of a mere blow job. Challenge accepted, and stakes secured, Iceberg's bitch proceeded to give a blow job so great that the rival pimp came within just a few minutes, losing the bet with pleasure and astonishment. I had long wished to experience such a transcendental blow job.

I procured two eighths of crack instead of one, just in case, and invited Sin to the back room with me. When I emerged later that evening, high enough to greet passing jetliners, I had come twice, courtesy of one quick and dizzying blow job and one fuck. Worth every nugget of crack and more.

"I hope it's okay for me to suggest this," I said to Lusi, thinking quickly on my feet, "but, what if I pay you for the night? That way you don't have to worry about customers, and we can continue our conversation. Maybe we can leave here and go swim at my hotel or something?" I was reduced to a shy boy, plying a prostitute back to my hotel under the guise of a midnight swim. I was already in deep for her. It didn't matter that her profession was older than religion. She could have been a serial killer, and it wouldn't have mattered. I'd have spent my nights brainstorming romantic-comedy-worthy proposals to her either way.

"I happy you ask this." She had her hands clasped around the back of my neck now. "I give discount. Because I like you. Only five hundred thousand."

"Sold."

"What sold?"

"I agree to your negotiations."

"Funny man. I like."

At my hotel I gave her a pair of shorts "for swimming" and she laughed and dropped them on the floor.

"Baby," she whispered, "I want make love for you."

She allowed me to undress her slowly and I tried to contain my awe at each step. Her dark, satin skin, like fine sheets I'd be happy to spend a coma in. Her perky breasts, deep purple nipples. Her flat, tight stomach. Her gazelle-like legs. She was a specimen, and I was painfully ready for her.

She insisted that I allow myself to finish, though I wasn't convinced that she had. I wondered if that was just a professional precaution for her—never coming with customers. Even though it didn't feel like a professional exchange, I guessed it might have been for her. But I allowed myself to believe, in the moment, that what I felt was mutual, and within the neighborhood of real. I held her close, and we continued kissing, slowly, gently, our mouths just barely touching, the current of a nine-volt battery passing between our lips. Later, her hands commanded me to attention again. She climbed on top, and I watched her body move slowly against me, narrow beams of light wrapped her silhouette, patterned from the window shades like a Cucoloris effect in a 1950s noir film.

"Baby," she said, as if a question were bubbling to the surface, "you help me come now?" I was more than enthused to oblige and excited that she wanted me to do this for her. To venture beyond the professional arrangement. To share that level of intimacy. I turned her over and started working my way down her body until she pulled my head back up toward her face.

"Not like this, baby," she said through a coy smile.

"What would you like?" I asked.

"To the bathroom. There I come."

She laid herself in the bathtub and turned the shower massage handle to full blast, aimed at her vagina.

"Now you kiss here," she pointed to her breasts, "and lick."

I had no issues with kissing or licking her anywhere, especially not there, so I did as I was told. She held the showerhead between her thighs as water rebounded off of her crotch and spritzed the air around us. She moaned lightly and squeezed my arm until she said, like a simple matter of fact, "Okay baby. I come already."

"Really? Wow. I barely noticed."

"Thank you."

"Anytime. But, you didn't like having sex with me? Did I do something wrong? Can I do anything better? I don't mind if you tell me." I was nervous. I wanted to be enough for her.

"You make love good, baby. I like. But to come very hard for me."

"Because . . ." I was hesitant to ask but I wanted to be open and honest with Lusi from the start. I wanted to know everything about her. "Is it because you've been with so many men . . . for work?"

"No, baby. Is true, I do with many man for work. But don't worry. When I marry, I get the surgery."

"The surgery?"

"Yes. To make like virgin again. More tight. The pussy, baby. If you marry me, heh heh heh, I get the surgery."

"Well, I'll keep that in mind," I said, barely able to process everything at once. "But . . . so what's the problem with you coming then?"

"When I young, my family. They cut off," she said.

"What? They cut what off?" I'd heard of that reversal surgery before, and I was aware that they had perfected it in Southeast Asia especially. But she seemed, well, naturally lubricated on the inside. I didn't understand how that could be possible. I was so confused. And felt an irrational sense of guilt about decisions I had not yet made. I always considered myself to be open-minded. I fell for her before I knew she could be a lady boy. What kind of man would I be to turn on her now? What about her past would change the perfect chemistry between us? I squeezed her hand in solidarity. I was ready for her to reveal herself to me and for all that it might entail.

"The clit," she said, to my strange relief. "Because I Muslim. They cut off when I little girl."

"Holy shit. I'm so sorry," I said, somewhat horrified again after recalibrating my thoughts.

"It's okay, baby. You help me come. Now we both feel good. You want sleep?"

We settled into bed and our limbs wound together like nesting rattlesnakes. Allowing the light, gentle sound of Lusi's breath to carry me into a trance, I drifted off, thinking about all there was in the world that I would never understand. I wondered what I was doing in my life, in the suburbs of New York, while Lusi's family was holding her down, taking a knife to her clitoris, denying her a lifetime of maximum pleasure in the name of faith. I vowed to give her everything she'd never had. A life flashed through my mind. Lusi, wanting for nothing. Beautiful, healthy children, cared for, educated, raised without lies, without god, without any rules other than the ones that had to do with kindness and compassion, allowed to keep their sensitive parts, never knowing what it would be like having to sandblast their way to completion in the bathtub of a hotel in paradise. If I ever have a daughter, I thought, she will be highly orgasmic, like a normal Indonesian girl. His will be damned.

CHAPTER 17

"I love you." I couldn't believe I'd said it. Lusi's pupils expanded, but the rest of her face paused with restraint. I thought about it for another moment to make sure that I meant it. How could I? We'd spent two days together, barely leaving my hotel except for an occasional meal and an evening walk along the beach. It had been less than forty-eight hours since we'd met, albeit the best hours of my life. I'd told girlfriends I loved them before but never this soon and, honestly, there was never any truth to it. It always seemed like the right time to say it. But in this case with Lusi, this wasn't the love that feels required after a certain amount of time invested in a relationship. It was the love one hears about. The kind you never believe is real until it's so real you can't stand it. The punch in the gut and all of those other clichés.

"I mean it. I love you," I said.

"Really?"

"Yes, really."

"I love you too, baby. I so happy for you." She slid on top of me and guided me inside of her without a condom. Afterward, we went to the bathroom together.

When she was finished, she looked up at me from the bathtub and asked, "Baby, today we go Waterbom?"

Waterbom was a water park Lusi had been telling me about. She said it was her favorite place in the world. I believed her, but it made me sad, knowing that she had seen so very little in the world. Surely there were better places than a water park to have as one's favorite place on earth. I also questioned the need for a water park of any kind on an island paradise, but I decided to approach it with an open mind.

Waterbom was a typical water park. Slightly smaller than Action Park in New Jersey but also not entirely unimpressive. It was a fine place. What caught my attention most, though, was how many conservative Muslim women were there, covered from head to toe. I wondered how they'd be able to swim in any enjoyable way. Or if they were there to watch. To be tortured by the heat while their husbands and sons enjoyed the indescribable pleasure of being projected at high speeds through overly chlorinated water.

Lusi and I went to the coed lockers area and changed. I noticed a million eyes on us. On her, mostly. Sometimes on me, to confirm that I was with her, and then, ultimately, back to her. A blatant tease to the married men with their shadow wives. Part of me felt guilty. But I also felt proud. I was with this girl. The one they all went home to dream of. The one their martyrs wished to see when greeted by virgins in heaven. Let them look, I thought, so that when they find nothing but disappointment in the afterlife they'll have the memory of this vision that is Lusi to get them through eternity.

To my surprise, many of the women changed into what I learned were burkinis: burkas in bathing suit form. It made me feel better for them, knowing they'd be able to join in the fun. What a drag to go down a waterslide covered in such a way, but better than the sidelines, I concluded.

The women glanced toward Lusi more than the men did. The men attempted to be subtle. They tried to hide their gazes. But the women were not subtle. They stared without shame. She embodied everything they hated and everything they wished they could be. I found it difficult to take the same satisfaction in their stares as I did in the men's. Theirs came from a deeper place, one where people spent lifetimes convincing themselves that subjugation, obedience, and servitude were spiritual preferences. But little did they know what they and Lusi had in common, that she too abstained from alcoholic consumption because she was a good Muslim girl. She was one of them, if not exactly in the way they would have preferred her to be.

We went on every slide at Waterbom several times. A smile danced across Lusi's face the entire day. She radiated a joy that I'd never known myself. Such simple pleasures, I thought, are what life is all about. What love is all about. I was an expert, all of a sudden, in the most tacky clichés available. And tacky clichés, I thought, are also what life is all about. "God Only Knows" by the Beach Boys played on a loop in my mind.

As the day went on, the lines for the waterslides grew longer. We decided to grab a pair of yellow tubes and float freely along the artificial moat that encircled the park. Lusi and I held hands and took turns swinging one another toward the walls, splashing and laughing the whole time. We'd pass people at one stretch, and those same people would pass us at another. I saw some women in their burkinis whom I recognized from the lockers area. The sting in their gazes had turned to delight. They were ensconced in too much goodness, too absorbed in the now to remember what they were supposed to disapprove of. When the teachings and the history and the pressure of their god were all stripped away, this was who they were: human beings, lost in the joy of floating in cool water on a hot day.

That night I woke up to Lusi getting dressed.

"What are you doing?" I asked.

"You sleep, baby. I go work now. Morning I come back."

I sat up. "What? Work? You mean, like . . . work?"

"Yes, baby. My mamasan. She call me. She angry I no work. I have to work now or mamasan be more angry."

"Well, fuck her!"

"No, baby. I fuck you, heh heh heh. She make big trouble for me I no work. Sleep, baby. I go work. I come back morning."

CHAPTER 18

I woke up to a knocking on my door. It was Lusi. She was wearing the same dress she had worn the night we met. She jumped at me with a hug and a deep kiss. I was beyond thankful to taste toothpaste.

"Baby, I miss you. I think of you all night with customer."

"Is that so?"

"Yes. Is true, baby."

"Well, I should be happy to hear that, right? I thought of you all night too. In my dreams. But I wasn't with a customer."

"Heh heh heh. You joke. Funny. But look." She jumped on my bed and pulled a wad of rupiah out of her purse. "Look all this money!" It was like the scene from *Indecent Proposal* but with much less money. I tried to be supportive.

"Wow. That is a lot," I said. "No need for details on how you made it though."

"Baby, I so smart. You know what I do?" She was going to tell me the details. "I meet the man who ask 'you suck my friend dick and I fuck ass?' and he wants

133

pay me double." Her impression of the man's voice, cartoon-monster deep, was very cute, all considered.

"He wanted to fuck his friend's ass?" I asked hopefully.

"No, baby. My ass. He not the gay man, baby."

"I can wish, can't I?"

"Why you wish he gay, baby?" she asked. I shrugged. She continued, "But I say, 'no, this not double, this special so this three time money.' And he say okay. Good, right, baby? Smart? Now I show mamasan I work three night and only work one. And I spend two night more only you!" She punctuated that with another kiss and a handful of my crotch. It was the most romantic thing a girl had ever done to find a way to spend more time with me.

"I am kind of proud of you. And I'm excited you're here now."

"Heh heh heh. I feel you excited."

After having sex in a way that felt like what I always imagined love was supposed to feel like, we saw to Lusi's orgasm, showered together, and then cocooned ourselves in the bedsheets for several hours. For the first time in longer than I could remember I felt present in my life as it was happening. Nothing was on my mind but the feel of Lusi's skin against mine. Finally, her voice crept through the silence, "Baby?"

"Yes, my love?"

"Yesterday, thank you for you go with me to Waterbom. So much fun with you."

"Thank you for taking me. It was a really wonderful time for me too."

"Good. But I think, maybe today . . . I take you somewhere for you. Anywhere in Bali you want we go."

"Oh. That's so sweet."

"Yes. I taste sweet, right? Heh heh heh."

"You do. And I have an idea. Is there anywhere you know that's like, one of the beautiful beaches where the surfers always talk about? I've always heard of the legendary surfing in Bali, and I've never seen anything like that. Maybe that would be nice to see while I'm here."

"Yes! I know! Uluwatu. Very beautiful. With the cliff. And the cave. And big, big waves for the surfer. But maybe dangerous to surf there, baby."

"That sounds perfect. And don't worry. I won't surf there. I just want to see it. I want to feel it."

"Feel the sand there? At the beach?"

"Well, sure. But I mean, the energy. You know? A place like that must have a certain energy to it."

"Yes, baby. I understand. I think Uluwatu does have this. You will see."

The ride to Uluwatu was an adventure in itself. Sitting behind Lusi on her motorbike, my life flashed before my eyes several times as she'd turn back to smile at me, barely noticing the oncoming traffic coming around treacherous turns ahead. My only protection was a 1930s biker helmet that Lusi had picked out for me at a local motorbike shop. She said I looked very handsome in it, and that was enough for me, though at certain times throughout the ride I did question the logic. In the end, she negotiated the route without incident, if not without several near misses.

When we arrived, I was happy to touch solid ground with all limbs intact. We parked next to a van with some surfers just packing up to leave, and I could tell by their expressions that this was the place I hoped it would be. The blissful exhaustion on their faces spoke volumes, and they seemed to be in such introspective states that they only gave half glances to Lusi in her short-shorts and tight tank top. It was as if their male reflexes required them to look, but their libidos and, maybe more so, their spirits, had yet to come back to earth after their morning dance with Poseidon.

Lusi and I worked our way down a steep cliffside, and I wondered how the surfers had made it up and down this path with surfboards in tow. I made the last leap down to sand and caught Lusi as she jumped at me, laughing.

We ambled through a series of open caves and a stretch of beach opened up in front of us, with a view of the surf I had been hoping for. Despite my anticipation, I was in awe. The waves were not enormous but were perfectly shaped, like those Japanese paintings that hang in so many freshman dorm rooms.

Suddenly, I wished to be a veteran surfer, to know what it felt like to have that power beneath my feet, thrusting me forward toward land, pulsing through me like it recognized my molecules as having come from the dust of the same stars that have nurtured its strength over millennia. I wanted to transcend myself and lose all sense of time in the foam of the sea. Less than fifty feet in front of me, a long-haired teen in a neon-yellow wet suit, looking so confident and proud atop a wave, was swept under, crushed, and pummeled. He emerged holding his ribs, the pain on his face evident as he staggered toward the shore. I wanted nothing more than to feel the pain he felt.

"Ooh!" Lusi exclaimed. "He look so hurt."

We watched him drag his way to safety and tend to his wounds. Rushing to check on him, his friends encircled him tentatively. After some inaudible deliberation they patted him on the back and together, they all picked up their boards, walked calmly toward the water, and paddled out for more.

"Crazy. Right, baby?"

"Yeah, crazy. And beautiful. It's like he's beyond human out there."

"Yes. Maybe. More than the human. Like the superman, right, baby?"

"Exactly." I grabbed her to pull her in for a kiss, and she pulled away. "What's wrong?" I asked.

"People look." She motioned back to the beach. I hadn't realized how far we'd wandered out. It was still shallow quite far out from the beach, and we were both so lost in it all that we'd just kept walking toward the surf without thought. Of the few people back on the beach, a couple of surfers recuperating from their exertions and some men and women tanning, maybe three or four of them actually were looking in our direction. Still, it seemed more likely they were taking in the swells beyond us.

"Are you serious? I don't think they care."

"But if you kiss me they see. I shy."

I bit my tongue, smiled, took her hand, and we walked back to the southern edge of the beach toward some small caves. I pulled her into one, and she warmly accepted my kisses there after taking one last look to see if we were within anyone's eyesight. We sat down against a boulder and held each other, alternating between kissing and napping, occasionally talking in between. We shared stories of our childhoods and some from our more recent pasts. She told me about her job, in somewhat more detail than I might have liked to have known about someone I was in love with. Stories about girth and length, about positions of varying comfort levels, about experimental couples, about role playing requests, and even a few about Indonesian celebrities. Finally, I asked the one question about her career to which I actually wanted to know the answer.

"How did you first start doing this? This kind of work?"

"How I become prostitute?"

"Yes."

"I meet my mamasan for first time, she tell me I have very sexy body and many men will like. I say her thank you. And she say I can make the good money if I the prostitute for her. I want the money so much, baby, but I scared because I don't want to upset Allah. I want to be the good Muslim girl. But I remember my Imam, when I little, he say, if you have the sex before married, it same-same like being the prostitute. And I already have the sex with a boy from my village. He fuck me, baby, even if I don't want. You understand, baby?"

"Yes. I think I understand." In my heart I wanted to believe that even her god would not equate the act of rape with what her Imam had meant. I quickly realized I was giving too much credit to any god.

She continued, "I say to my mamasan, 'I think it is okay, because I already have the sex.' When I try for first time I do with the nice, handsome man from Australia. And when he gives me the money I am so happy. My mamasan say I very good girl. And she give me her magic so I make more and more money. This is how, baby."

"Her magic?" I asked, almost numb to having my mind blown by new information.

"To help for more customers. She has the magic for me and more customer want me and pay me more."

"I don't see how it's possible that just letting people see you wouldn't bring in all the business you can handle."

"Heh heh heh. Thank you, baby. But only for Western man my look help."

"Indonesians don't like the way you look?"

"Not always, baby. They say I too dark. My lips too thick."

"They're idiots. You're lips are perfection."

"But Indonesia man no like. They say like the black girl, my skin and lips. Even though I not black girl. But my skin very dark. And these lips . . ." She puckered them out for me to examine. They looked like lips I could kiss for a long time.

"First of all, what the hell is their problem with black girls? And second of all, I love your lips. I'll take your lips forever."

"Heh heh heh. You take them, baby? Just my lips. In your suitcase when you go back Jakarta?"

"Yes. All of you. Every inch. I want to take all of you back with me. Which reminds me, I need to buy a new suitcase at some point. But I don't want to think of going back right now. Honestly, I don't want to be anywhere but right here ever again."

"But baby, at night the water come here. I think we die if we stay here."

"Okay. But let's be here now. For as long as we can."

"Okay, baby. You love it here with me now, right, baby?"

"I do. I really do love it here with you right now. But, can we get back to this magic business? What's that all about, exactly?"

"Oh. My mamasan. She give me the magic. So the Indonesian man want me."

"I got that, I think. But, you're telling me this is real? I didn't think that could be real."

"Yes, real, baby. When I first am working, no Indonesia man want me. Many foreigner but sometime when no foreigner, mamasan want me to find Indonesia man for customer. And then mamasan, she give me the magic and my Indonesia customer start more."

"I'm not sure how to feel about that."

"Why, baby?"

"Well, how do I know you didn't use magic on me? What if I don't really like you?" I asked, teasingly.

"Heh heh heh. Baby, you funny. The magic mamasan gave is for the Indonesia man. Not for you."

We brushed the sand off of each other and meandered along the caves toward the main path. As we walked, practically skipping, we both suddenly stopped at the same exact time. In a smaller cave sat a Buddhist monk in his full crimson garb. He gave off what I can only describe as an aura. It was palpable, almost visible. It extended beyond his cloth and reverberated within the cave. Its edges framed him perfectly, as if he had been there for thousands of years. His presence, like water against stone, had smoothed out an architecture for itself.

Neither Lusi nor I spoke. All that needed to be said was communicated between our clasped hands as the world aligned itself for our benefit. In complete sync with each other, we stood observing this man's transcendence, the aquatic clapping of earth's magnetic forces to our backs. His nirvanic stillness provoked a heightened awareness in me to the intensity and frailty of it all. It was clear that he knew one thing better than any of us: none of it would last.

CHAPTER 19

I'd been back in Jakarta for two weeks before Lusi joined me. I met her at the airport and hugged her and instinctually went to kiss her until she reminded me that people look. I took her hand and walked her to the car, where Rahim awaited. He greeted her like the gentleman he is, and she smiled coyly. During the ride home she said she was tired and placed her head in my lap and dozed off. When Iron Maiden's "Caught Somewhere in Time" queued on the tape player, I asked Rahim to make it louder.

"Just a little bit louder. So we don't wake her."

"Yes, Paul."

When the song ended, Rahim turned the tape player down.

"Paul, you happy now?" he asked softly, taking me by surprise.

"I am, Rahim. Thanks for asking."

"I can see. Your face is changed."

"Well, that's good for everyone, isn't it?"

"Good for you, Paul. Only important good for you."

Once Lusi had showered and unpacked, I showed her the garden, which she liked very much. She asked if she could plant some flowers, and the metaphor of her wanting to plant roots in my home seemed like life fulfilling its grand promise. We stood by the edge of the water, and I slowly took her clothes off. Then I took my clothes off and held her close and tight and threw us both into the water.

We splashed around for a while and then she put her arms around my neck and held her face in front of mine.

"This is most happy I am, more than ever, Paul."

"I'm so glad to hear that. I feel the exact same way."

I grabbed two hands full of her tight ass and pulled her close to me. I wanted to make love to her, but I wasn't hard yet. I guided one of her hands down to help, but nothing happened. I wondered if I was overexcited, if that was such a thing. I can't say I'd never in my life been slow to become erect, but it usually involved ungodly amounts of cocaine and liquor. Now, I was as sober as I'd been in years.

"Maybe we should go inside," I said. "I think I'm too wound up. Let's just go relax in the bed."

"Okay, baby," Lusi replied with hesitation.

In the bedroom it didn't get any better. I was ashamed and furious but didn't want her to think anything was wrong so I tried to go down on her until she reminded me that such things didn't work for her.

"Something wrong, baby? We don't make love?" she asked with disappointment.

"No. I think I'm just overwhelmed that you're here. I've never felt this way before. Maybe I'm just all mixed up or something."

"Baby, I had a bad feeling for this," she said, not looking me in the eye.

"No, Lusi. I promise. It's just—I don't know what it is but it's nothing to worry about. Trust me."

"But something happen, baby. I think this why."

"What is why?" I asked.

"My mamasan."

"Oh, fuck her, Lusi."

"But baby. You cannot fuck her. You have to listen. She do this, I think."

"What? What are you talking about?"

"Baby, when I leave I tell my mamasan that I leave for you. She tell me if I go she curse you."

"Excuse me?"

"Okay, baby. But she say she curse you and maybe she mean you lose money or I don't know but maybe this how she curse you and now we don't have no sex."

"You think that I'm not getting hard right now because your mamasan is upset that you left?"

"She very angry, baby. Because she give me the magic and I leave to live Jakarta with you. She say she take your magic and she curse you."

"You're serious? My magic?"

"Yes, baby. I don't lie to you with this. I want to see you so much. I love you, baby. You know. But maybe this the bad idea. Maybe I make you like this."

I was boiling inside but tried to remain rational. On one hand, I no longer underestimated this country. On the other hand, it simply couldn't be.

"Lusi, let's just relax. We can go for dinner and have a few drinks . . ."

"But baby, you know I no drink because I Muslim," she interrupted.

"Yes, I remember. I'll have a few drinks. We'll eat. And we'll come home and make love."

"Oh, I hope so, baby."

CHAPTER 20

I sat in my office, feeling defeated. "Half the Man I Used to Be" by the Stone Temple Pilots played on my "High School Favorites" playlist. I had it on repeat, and my newly purchased hi-fi computer speakers really brought out the heroin-induced sadness in the vocals. I had always believed that the great equalizer among men was the ability to fuck. It was the reason that neither Bill Gates nor Shaquille O'Neal would ever be any more a man than my friend out my window in the village across the moat. As long as a man could fuck, he was as much a man as any. But on this day, I felt like less a man than most.

I'd spent several hours the night before Googling "erectile dysfunction," and when I woke up I didn't even want to try to have sex. I didn't want to go through the humiliation of failure yet again. Lusi carried on about her mamasan. She was convinced it was a curse. She felt at fault for my lack of manhood. But according to Google it could have been caused by one of many psychosomatic issues, most of which could be cured by one therapy or another. Also according to Google, while black magic was widely practiced in this part of the world, the scientific community almost unanimously agreed that there was no proof of it.

Out the window, my friend was digging a hole behind his hut. He used a pickax, and I was impressed by his form. How did he know to bend at the knees that way? His movements were efficient and precise. Perhaps such things were instinctual to real men. He couldn't possibly have had any formal schooling nor the benefit of a Google search and yet there he was, full of knowledge and ability. I wondered if a professional athlete like Mike Tyson, or a man of knowledge, wisdom, and experience like Richard Branson, would have had the instinctual ability to wield a pickax against the earth with such form. The thought simultaneously angered me and made me proud. The anger was rooted in jealousy. The pride, in the thought that my friend could out-man the titans of the universe. When all the riches and rewards of intellectual pursuits were gone, this man would out-man everyone. Then it occurred to me that I had never seen him with a wife. No woman ever entered or left his hut. What a waste of ability. I wondered if I could somehow send a prostitute to him. I was convinced he would fuck the living shit out of her. Like a man.

"Have you given him a name yet?" Nisa inquired as she entered my office.

"He's not a pet, Nisa. He's a man," I snapped back in a tone I'd never used with her.

"I was joking, Paul. I'm sorry. Should I come back later?"

"No. I'm sorry." I exhaled. "You just caught me by surprise. Deep in thought. Not the best mood today."

"Really? That's so surprising. I know that Lusi arrived this weekend. You were so excited last week. I imagined there would be rainbows and butterflies floating around you today."

"That's quite romantic of you to say, Nisa." We made eye contact and laughed. It was my first smile of the day, and it felt good. "I'm happy that Lusi's here. But . . . well, it's complicated."

"Isn't that what adults always say about love?"

"Nisa, you are becoming quite the wiseass lately."

"Maybe I spend too much time with you."

"Maybe. I should thank you for making her travel arrangements though."

"It's my job, Paul."

"No. It isn't. But I do appreciate it."

"It's my pleasure, Paul," she assured me.

I looked back out the window and asked her, "Do you think he has a woman in his life? Or a man, for that matter? I don't want to assume, I guess. But you know what I mean. There are kids in that village. None seem to be his. So people obviously get together. But—"

"I really am not an expert, Paul," she interrupted. "But if I understand what you're getting at, no, he doesn't seem to have anyone. Even though in most cases with the poor like that, they would have something arranged through family. Maybe he just hasn't been lucky yet. Or has nothing to offer."

"Nothing to offer, my ass."

"What?"

"Nothing." I rearranged some papers on my desk. "I was thinking, what if we hired a prostitute and sent her to him . . . I just want him to have what other men have."

"Prostitute?" She was incredulous.

"Well, I can see how that comes off."

"And 'we'? '*We*' will hire a prostitute? Really, Paul?"

"I'm not trying to offend you. I certainly don't associate you with anything that you might see as indecent. But I'd need a local to help me facilitate the transaction."

"Paul, you are hilarious sometimes. Just so you know, I'm more open-minded than some locals. I am not blind to reality. Men in Indonesia hire prostitutes. Local men even more so than Westerners."

"Really?"

"Yes, really. And to be honest with you, Paul, I know about Lusi."

"Wait. What? But when I first met her, I . . . how? She told you? Do others know?" I was disarmed entirely. A strange dread washed over me.

"Don't worry. Your secret is safe. She told me when I spoke with her on the phone to help make her arrangements. Let's just say we talked about a lot of things. And I actually admire you."

"What?"

"Paul, it's okay. Every man who comes to this country sleeps with a prostitute. Married men too. But very few of them see the prostitute as a person. Lusi told me that you didn't know about her when you met. And you didn't judge her when you found out. You got to know her. You saw her inside. And you weren't insecure, knowing how many other men . . . well . . ."

"I think I get your point," I finally said. "But, can we get back to my friend and his cause? The professional arrangement?"

"Okay, Paul. The professional answer is 'no.' There is very little I wouldn't do for you. But I can't arrange that. Please understand." Then she followed a brief silence with, "You won't be upset with me?"

"No, of course. I have enough to be upset about. It was just a thought. I shouldn't have asked. Let's forget it?"

"I'm starting to appreciate your thinking, in strange ways," she said with a compassionate smile. "Would now be a good time to discuss advertising?"

Later that day I had several creative reviews. I was impressed with what the teams had accomplished. I liked the shifts I noticed in their thinking. Everything I saw felt exactly right for the respective assignments. All of the ideas were deeply rooted in local insights. One campaign in particular, for an Indonesian dairy company, was downright inspiring. It involved an animated milk droplet navigating its way throughout a series of commercials. In each "episode," the milk droplet conquered various comical stumbling blocks on its way up and out the straw of a milk pack. It was a concept I believed would resonate quite well with kids.

The client was excited about the campaign and only slightly hesitant. When I told them I had so much faith in the campaign that I would talk to some acquaintances at Pixar Studios about producing the series, they quickly came around. I riffed on merchandising potential beyond milk sales. I even made up an idea on the spot for a milk droplet app, with a gamified rewards system, that would motivate kids to fast without complaint during Ramadan. The parents in the room nodded and joked about their kids always complaining during fast, and all of the young creatives in the room joked about how it would have gotten them to shut up and behave during such times.

Before we left, the client pulled me and the account director to the side, verbally committed double the budget they had originally planned, reiterating their appreciation and excitement.

Two hours and several kilometers later I was home. Lusi was in the kitchen with Tetti, and the scent that greeted me made my mouth water instantly. Turning, Tetti noticed me, gave a little giggle, and scurried out of the room. I walked over to kiss Lusi. "What was that about?"

"Oh, heh heh," Lusi laughed. "Tetti is embarrass."

"Why would she be embarrassed to see me?"

"Because she help me to cook special meal. Good for man. To make the sex more." She grabbed my balls and kissed me.

"Did you really tell Tetti that I had problems getting a hard on?"

"Hard on? It means dick hard?"

"Yes, dear. It means dick hard."

"Heh heh," she laughed and hugged me. "It's okay, baby. I told her my mamasan curse you. She understand but still maybe shy. But she told me that her cousin has the curse also. And the aunt of Tetti made this and the curse go away. She help me make for you, baby. Exciting, right?" I couldn't deny that her enthusiasm alone should have turned me on.

"If it works, then it will be exciting." I watched her stir the pot. "Do I want to know what's in it?"

"No, baby. Maybe you don't know. You just eat."

"Okay. I'll go shower. When it's ready to eat you let me know."

I practically licked the bowl clean. Partly because I wanted the remedy to work. Partly because it really did taste very good. I made a mental note to look into branding and marketing it at some point. The world's first, true, over-the-counter ED remedy.

After dinner I suggested that we go to a movie to take our minds off of things. Lusi chose the film. I noticed too late that it was directed by Danny Allen and was a basic cut-and-paste of everything he'd done previously.

It was about a special forces unit trapped behind enemy lines with no choice but to kill hundreds of Muslims as they worked their way back to safety. Beyond the killing, phrases such as "towel heads," "sand niggers," and "Muslim terrorist scum" were employed. There was even a sex scene, obviously edited by local censors, after which one of the main characters commended his sexual conquest for not being "as fucked up as all your fellow rag-tops." For reasons beyond my critical taste in cinema, I was uncomfortable with many of the film's choices.

Hiding my head as we exited, I asked Lusi, "So, what did you think?"

"Good movie. So much explosions, heh heh," was her reply. Then, because there hadn't been enough irony in the day, "But I worry, so much the bad cursing. This is bad if the kids see, no?"

"Don't worry. I won't let our kids see it," I assured her.

"Heh heh. You want we have kids?" She squeezed my hand tighter but didn't make advances beyond that, because "people look."

"Well, let's go home and have sex. And we'll see if any kids come from it."

Her smile lit up the night.

"And baby," she said.

"Yes, dear?"

"Tonight when we have sex. Even if you have more problem from the curse, we go to bathtub and I come?"

"We'll do both. For sure."

CHAPTER 21

"Dude. That is really fucked up," was Jeff's reaction when I confided in him my recent issues. "Have you tried medication?"

We were at his lounge, having some man-to-man talk. It had been over a month since Lusi arrived in Jakarta.

"I've tried everything I could think of and then some. Pills. The blue and the yellow. Separately. Together. Random exercises I found online. Visualization. Lusi and Tetti made me a special dish that's supposed to help. Nothing."

"Oh, I had that shit once. Tastes baller though, right?"

"It was delicious. I thought of starting a restaurant based around it. Or packaging it for global distribution."

"The locals wouldn't like that," Jeff said. "That's some bad juju to mess with right there. And you've already had enough tangling with the locals, my friend."

"Fair point. Better to keep my head down."

"Now we just need to figure out how to keep your little head up," Jeff said through a proud and cheesy smirk.

"Who's having trouble keeping their little head up?"

Scotty appeared out of nowhere. "Are you guys drinking the good shit? What's up, my American homeboys?"

We both greeted him, only half trying to hide our disappointment. Jeff nodded to the bartender to bring another glass. No getting out of it at this point.

"So what's this?" Scotty asked. "What about not keeping it up? You, Goldberg? I heard you brought a lady back from Bali? If she looks anything like the last chick I banged in Bali I'd think the problem would be keeping it down. You know what I'm saying? It's like, 'Get down, boy! Get on down, ya hear?' " He pointed the demands at his crotch as if disciplining a schnauzer.

"I've been cursed," I finally conceded, if for no better reason than to shut him up. "Some witch doctor mama-san madam didn't want me bringing Lusi back to Jakarta and put a curse on me." I couldn't be any more humiliated anyway. I might as well see if Scotty had a solution.

Scotty laughed in a spit take, with a very expensive mouthful of liquor. He laughed until he caught his breath. Jeff and I looked at each other, annoyed.

"Oh, Goldberg. You fell in love with a hooker?" He finally got out in between breaths. "In Bali?"

Jeff's eyes encouraged me to stay calm.

"Well, it's not quite that simple," I started.

"Oh, I know, I know. You didn't know she was a hooker at first, right?"

I wanted to punch him. I just stared while he finished laughing again.

"Dude," he continued, "if I had a dollar for every Westerner who ended up with a hooker in Bali. Oh . . . my . . . but you are the *first* I have ever met who actually tried to take one home with him. *After* finding out she was a prostitute. Goldberg! You are amazing." Then he turned to Jeff, "Have you taught him nothing?"

"Scotty, be cool, man. He fell in love. It's happened to the best of us."

"Yeah, I fell in love, dude. And then I had sex with hookers. But I didn't fall in love with a hooker. Especially not a hooker from Bali."

"Hey Scotty, feel free to add anything helpful here," I said in an irrepressibly irritated tone that must have betrayed inner violence.

"Okay, okay. I'm sorry, man. This is juicy stuff. But lucky for you, my lady's great-aunt is into some black magic kind of hooey. She's told me stories about shit like this. So, let me guess. Your . . . lady . . ."

"Lusi," I offered.

"Right. Lusi . . . she was a . . . professional . . ." He looked at me for confirmation.

"Go on."

"And in Bali she had a mamasan who was less than pleased about her leaving . . ." He looked again, and I nodded. He went on, "And she put a curse on you that basically made it impossible for you to get a hard on as long as Lusi is here with you?"

"Yeah, Lusi told me that's more or less what was said."

"And you still went through with it?" Scotty asked, as if questioning a child who had stolen candy from a corner store.

"It was kind of after the fact. And I don't really believe that shit. Well, I didn't believe that shit." They were both staring at me, waiting for the conclusion. "I guess now I believe that shit. I kind of have to."

"You have to send her back," Jeff quickly concluded.

"Fuckin' A right you have to send her back," Scotty jumped in. "Put that sweet hooker ass on the next plane back to Bali. Like, immediately." Jeff grabbed his arm, letting him know to tone it down.

"What if I just hire another witch doctor to reverse the curse?" I was grasping. "Maybe your great aunt-in-law or whoever that is, Scotty?"

"Dude, you do not want to fuck with these things. You have no idea what kind of shit you could stir up mixing curses. It's like the beams in *Ghostbusters*. You do not want to experiment with crossing curse beams. Haven't you had enough trouble already?"

My silence was answer enough, and he must have felt he was on a roll. "Seriously, man. You send her back. You put her on a plane. Get a good night's sleep. Then you go right out and hate fuck a few of these local girls. Prostitutes, local chicks, maybe even some white backpacker chicks. Just fuck away and live happily ever after like the ad king you're supposed to be here."

I looked through him with fury, but Jeff agreed.

"He's right, Paul. You should ask her to go back. If for no other reason, just to see what happens."

"All I heard was 'fuck away' and 'happy ever after.' Sounds like my kinda party. You mates wanna pour me a drink and fill me in?" Justin had just shown up, all smiles. It eased the tension in the room, and I settled on deferring the decision until the morning.

"I'll buy you a drink, mate," I said to Justin with a smile. "Especially since it's free. Right Jeff?" Shelving the serious talk, we let Justin entertain us with various anecdotes from his day. He relayed a pretty funny story about a horrific client meeting he was coming from. For the first time in my life I was happier to think about advertising over sex.

Later that night I told Lusi it might be a good idea for her to go home. I was drunk, but she was surprisingly on the same page otherwise.

"Baby, I think that also," she admitted. "Not good for you or for me like this."

"You'll be okay? Going back there?"

"Yes. I will be okay. It will be just like before. My mamasan will be happy if I back."

"I'll be sad to see you go."

"But maybe happy too. Because you have sex again, right? With another girl?"

"But I won't love her like you."

"What if she more beautiful than me? If you meet a girl like this, you tell me. And if I meet the other man I tell you. But I also go back to working now."

"I don't want to think about it right now. But I'll tell you if that happens."

"I hope so for you, baby. Even though then I be sad too." She hugged me.

"Hey Lusi. Why don't we go out to the pool? I'll make you come with the garden hose."

"Really, baby? Yes, I like."

After a few minutes of blasting Lusi with the hose and licking her firm nipples she squeezed my arm. "I come already, baby."

I turned the hose off and we fell asleep in spoon position on a patio chaise.

The next day, Lusi and I had a tearful goodbye at the airport. At the gate we held each other for eternities. I knew then that the love I felt for her was as real as I allowed myself to believe it was. The world had plotted against us in the cruelest of ways to force us apart. I'd never been under the false impression that there is only one true love in a person's life. But it had taken me close to thirty years to find one. I couldn't imagine how difficult it would be to find something similar again. I wondered to myself if sex was really worth more than love. Could I have lived with Lusi forever without making love to her? I didn't think that I only loved her for the sex, but I couldn't deny the inextricable importance of sex in love. Lusi had also told me that same morning that she couldn't imagine a life without sex, paid or unpaid. So, in the end, it wouldn't have mattered if I could live with her. She could not live with me. Not a single part of me blamed her for that. She deserved the level of intimacy that intercourse provides, if not the need to be brought to orgasm via high-pressure water cannon postsex.

Lusi and I kissed for the last time, and I kept my eyes closed long after it ended. I felt the palm of her hand brush against my cheek. I imagined her taking one last look, breathing me in for the final time and walking away. By the time I opened my eyes she was already being hit on by the Western hippie standing behind her in the security line. I turned and I walked to the car. When I got in Rahim asked if I wanted music, and I said I didn't. I wanted silence. What I got instead was the blaring, dissonant, combustion-engine cacophony of sound that is Jakarta traffic.

We were still another forty-five minutes from the house when I saw the beautiful, silk-framed face of a twentysomething girl in her pink hijab seated in the back seat of the car next to mine. I felt a light twitching in my crotch. I checked the time to see that it was five minutes past the time that Lusi's plane would have taken off. I raised my hand to meet my forehead and wondered if it could be that easy. Could it have been this stupid and simple, this Indonesian magic? I turned back to take in that porcelain-sculpted face again, separated from me by a couple of meters and two sheets of smog-glazed glass.

Within less than a minute of noticing her I was uncomfortably erect. I asked Rahim to pull into the only establishment I could see on the road ahead that might have a public restroom. It was a KFC. Without any semblance of guilt or concern for socially acceptable behavior, I quickly found myself in the dirty stall of the men's room with my hard dick in my hand. I started to imagine sex with Lusi but quickly realized I should steer clear of that goddamned curse. I tried to picture the girl I had just seen in the car, the girl who had inspired my first erection in the wake of that heinous spell, but the next female image that inserted itself into my head was that of Nisa.

Her deep dimples and easy smile projected clearly in my mind's eye. She was on top of me in my bed. We were both covered in sweat, and she cried out with great passion for Allah. Shocked but ready to go, I let it happen. Nisa, so sweet and pure. It felt inappropriate, but by the time I tried to envision somebody else, it was too late. I had already splatter-painted the bathroom wall with a month's worth of seed.

I opened my eyes and watched the globs of milky substance drip down over some wall scribblings. Something about the end of the infidel. Beneath that, a Dead Kennedys logo.

I looked around for toilet paper so that I might erase my existence from the tile and saw nothing but an empty cardboard tube. I left everything where it landed, washed my hands without drying them, and sauntered out of that restroom with a feeling of relief so profound it took the weight out of my walk.

CHAPTER 22

The next week was a blur of sexual encounters. I rented a room at the Four Seasons so that I could meet prostitutes there for lunch without my house staff judging me. At night I went to bars and clubs, taking home civilian women mostly and hiring professionals here and there for backup. I even went out with Scotty one night. I ran into him and the gang at Star Deli and he invited himself along with me to celebrate my return to sexual activity. I was reluctant, but he turned out to know some good places for meeting local girls and, for a married man, he knew a disturbing amount of the girls at those places.

I was exhausted every day, averaging two to three hours of sleep a night, but I was in such a good mood that it didn't slow me down at all. Work couldn't have been better. Our clients were all thrilled with the agency, and some of our best creative executions were hitting the public eye to rave reviews. Our planets of commerce were aligning.

Eric and I were invited to appear on a national talk show to discuss the success of the bank ads he had spearheaded. Apparently, the campaign slogan had struck a chord across the country and was becoming something of a cultural catch phrase. It was the banking version of "Get Juiced!" Initially flattered, I declined. I felt the language barrier would make for less entertaining television. I also thought it was a good idea to let the troops take their own victory laps. Eric clearly appreciated the gesture, and I got a televised mention. Nisa translated the footage for me the next morning as we watched on my laptop. He proclaimed that I was the best creative director in Indonesia and one of the best film directors in the Asia Pacific.

"He said that? Wow." I was stunned.

"Yes, Paul," Nisa assured me, "the staff, they start to really look up to you now. But, to be honest, it is also a sense of pride to make their boss look better than the bosses of others, even if not always true."

"Ah, so that's why they're laughing so much."

"Relax, boss. He is being genuine about you. But actually, Eric is very funny in Indonesian. He tells stories about agency life and the stereotypes of advertising people. The host asks if it is like this show 'The Madmen' and Eric says that there is less drinking and more praying because everyone is Muslim, except for the boss, who drinks and doesn't pray because he has no god." Nisa cracked up as she explained.

"That little shit said that?"

"He really did. But it was after he spoke so well of you. So maybe he is even?" She continued laughing.

"I'm gonna kill him."

"It's okay," she assured me through more laughter, "because he quickly changed the subject to jokes about account people. He says they are just as useless as in *Madmen* but not as well dressed."

"Oh my god. Is he coming in today?"

"Inshallah."

"Indeed. Well, maybe call him and tell him to take the day off. Just to be safe." We both laughed. Nisa put some papers in front of me that needed signing. Little arrow-shaped yellow stickies directed my hand to the correct signature lines, and I mechanically signed my name as we talked.

"I'm happy to see that your mood has changed for the better, Paul," she said, her eyes unerringly fixed to see that I signed the right places, stickies or not.

"It has, thank you. I mean, don't get me wrong. I miss Lusi. I really thought that might be it for me. But the world didn't see it the same way."

"Don't worry, Paul," she assured me, "the world might have more in store for you still. You are a good man, and you deserve a good woman who will love you."

"Who knows. For now I'll just do what I'm doing. Work is good. Life is back on track and—"

"Because you can have sex again?" she interrupted.

"What the hell, Nisa? Even you know about that? Couldn't you just pretend . . . just be cool about it?"

"It's not a big deal, Paul. But I'm sorry. I thought it

was okay to talk about these things with you. Lusi told me why she had to leave. She felt bad for you. I'm sure that must have been a hard choice."

"Or not that *hard* a choice." I raised my eyebrows, waiting for her to get the innuendo.

"So, only you can joke?"

"Okay fine. But you can imagine why that would be a sore subject for me."

"Sure, but now that you're back in action, I'm sure your subject is already sore, no?" She mimicked my eyebrow raise back and then let a laugh burst out.

"You are such a brat. Do we have any more work to discuss?"

"Yes, Paul." She became serious and professional again. "You have a lunch meeting with Indra today, and Santi wants to come to discuss some things with you at eleven thirty."

"It's eleven forty now."

"I'm sure she'll be up shortly. I'll let you know when she arrives." With that, Nisa retrieved the stack of signed papers from my desk. She walked out and gave a quick glance back as she closed the door behind her. I was about to turn to check on my friend when I heard Santi's voice on the other side of the door. She and Nisa were laughing about something, and I clicked open an e-mail to appear busy.

Nisa popped her head in and addressed me in an affected, hyperprofessional tone, "Mr. Paul, Santi has arrived for your appointment. Shall I send her in?"

"Yes, send her in, please," I said, playing along.

"Well, hello Mr. Paul, famous creative director!" Santi was overly bubbly and giving extra energy to every word she uttered. "We are all so proud today after Eric's great interview. Even us little old useless account people who dress bad." She was smiling, but I couldn't figure out her angle.

"I'm sorry about that. I'm not sure why he said that. On this project especially, your team was instrumental in making it all happen," I professed. I left out the part about her initially resisting the idea.

She covered her mouth and giggled. "Oh, don't be so serious. I was joking now. I know Eric is the funny man. He jokes always. And I think maybe in Bahasa Indonesia it is funnier than in English. You should be proud."

"Well, thanks then. You too. So what can I do for you?"

"Actually, it is what I can do for you." She tilted her head in a way that felt flirtatious, and I hoped that she wasn't about to offer me sexual favors. She had the look in her eyes. I didn't see how it was possible, but nothing would have surprised me anymore. I looked to the door and realized that she had closed it upon entering. I stared hard at the doorknob, trying to pry it open through telekinesis. I prayed with futility for the calls to prayer. Anything to avoid what I thought was about to happen. She continued, "I hear that you had a girlfriend from Bali but she went back already?"

A slow torture. She was now leaning her elbows on the desk across from me. Her great, cavernous cleavage called to me from close range. For lack of better options, I answered, "Yes. That's right." I pictured it all in my head. First, what would most likely be an excellent blow job. Then very rough sex. Then claims of rape. Then death squads. Or, I'd muster the strength to turn her down. She'd be insulted. Stories would be born. Threats would be made. Insults would be traded. Then death squads. Wanting to feel things out with caution, I followed with, "Why do you ask?"

Now her hand was on my hand. I didn't advance, but I didn't retreat. I tried not to sweat, out of concern that my dampness might be misinterpreted. My posture remained still. I knew that whatever happened in this moment would be worth writing about. My mental pad and pen were at the ready as she answered, "Well, as it turns out, Paul, I have a beautiful cousin who has recently moved back to Jakarta from Surabaya, and she is single. She wants to meet the good man and I instantly thought I should introduce her to you. What do you think?"

My mind put its pen down. "Are you serious?"

"Why shouldn't I be serious?" Santi asked, seriously.

My brain was twisting inside of itself. Was she fucking with me? Could the water have receded so far under the bridge that it had eroded her memory? Was this not the same former groupie whose merchant-of-death husband wanted to kill me for saying "the fuck" to his wife?

She thought it would be a good idea to set me up with her cousin? To bring me into the family? Would her husband be the best man at my wedding? Would he and I become friends? Would I be forced to become Muslim? Would all of life's ironies wrap themselves in a cute little bow for me?

I turned in my chair and looked out the window to my friend. He was squatting in the shade of a tree, peeling some sort of tropical fruit I'd never seen before. I wished he could be with me to hear what I was hearing. I wondered what he'd think about it. How would my friend advise me?

"Paul," he might say, "to find the good wife from the good family is difficult. Yes, they have wronged you. But you have wronged them by saying 'the fuck' with one of their own. Even is even now. Water is under bridge, as you Americans say. And they make amends by presenting you with one of their women. You cannot say no. This would be an insult to them. And to me as well. Because I would dream of having the wife from such a family. To deny this would be the sin against mankind."

I felt like he was being a little tough on me, even if this scene only existed in my mind, but he also might have had a point. Maybe it was time for me to open myself to possibility.

"Let me think about it," I said to Santi.

"Oh, really?" she responded with a broad smile. "I am so excited that you will think about this. No pressure, of course. But this is good. You let me know when you are ready."

"Okay. I will."

"And by the way, we are all very happy with the work here now. You are doing a great job, Paul. It's good that you are here."

"Thanks, Santi," I said, "That means a lot to me."

It did.

CHAPTER 23

A long and riotous night out with Jeff and Justin led to a Saturday morning flight to Phnom Penh. Jeff had been hired as a consultant for a fancy new club being opened by a Russian billionaire, Alexis, and his partner, Vadim, a highly decorated, retired special forces commander. According to Jeff, the place was going to be unlike anything we'd ever known. They were planning to call it the Jungle Club because, as Jeff said, "It's going to be totally fucking wild."

We arrived at our hotel just after 10:00 a.m., and Jeff slipped the manager a generous tip to arrange for an early check-in.

"Okay boys," he said, "have yourselves a nap and a shower. Order room service if you want. Have a drink. Whatever. We'll meet down here at one thirty and go to get some proper clothes before heading to the site. We've got a big night tonight."

"I thought the club ain't open yet, mate?" Justin stated as a question.

"It's not," Jeff answered. "But you know how it goes. Cambodia is the Wild West of the Wild West, man. We have to pay off the local mob boss. Make sure things stay smooth. So, he wants us to come to his underground spot and make a night of it. I think he really wants to get in with the Russians. They all play the game, ya know? He understands they could probably wipe him off the earth, but it'll be cheaper for them to use his security for the club. The trouble of a whole underworld overthrow would hardly be worth it."

"No, of course not. Even the underworld has a bottom line to think of," I said.

Jeff took us to a tailor he knew of. I purchased a swanky linen suit, Italian leather shoes, and a nice shirt. The salesgirl tried to sell me a Cuban-style hat, but I felt it was a bit much. Both Jeff and Justin went with the hats. We made it to the Jungle Club by 3:00 p.m., a half hour before Jeff had scheduled his meeting with Alexis and Vadim.

The entrance was grand, with platforms on either side of the walkway, I assumed for women to dance upon. The chains bolted to the marble raised some concerns.

"Bengal fucking tigers, homeboy," Jeff read my thoughts.

"No way, mate. Sure that's a good idea with drunk people in and out all night?" Justin asked.

"Probably not. But they wanted Bengal tigers. We spoke to someone from those tiger tour groups. They're getting a pair who couldn't make it in the wild. And they'll be drugged up like the ones all the annoying tourists pose with on Facebook. It's not 100 percent on the up and up, like most things around here. But I'll tell ya, these cats are going to be eating better than any tiger in any zoo anywhere in the world. I promise you that."

"Wagyu steak, huh?" I joked.

"Better. We're having live American elk shipped in. And we'll be broadcasting video footage in the club of the cats killing and eating their food in their 'play areas' earlier in the day."

"Whoa. That is pretty wild," I said.

"I see what you did there, mate." Justin punched me in the arm. "Always bringing the concepts back around."

"You are so on his nuts," Jeff said to Justin while slapping him lightly in the head and feigning a defensive, 1920s-era fisticuffs stance in front of him. Justin tackled Jeff to the ground, and they wrestled like teenagers. I leaned against a wall and wondered what my friends in Stonetown might have been doing at that moment. It's possible they, too, were play-fighting with one another. I wished they could be there in Cambodia with me, experiencing what I was experiencing. Then I heard a voice with a Russian accent, which surely could not have belonged to anyone from Stonetown.

"Jeffery," the voice, belonging to a man I'd later know as Vadim, called out in a slow, commanding manner, "you have to get the underhooks. You let him get control too easy. In real combat, with a real man, you are dead by now. Twice." Then a strange and boisterous laugh. The laugh of a man who had seen men die, possibly by his own hand.

Justin let Jeff up. They both straightened themselves out, and Jeff turned his internal dial up a notch for affect, "Vadim! Alexis! You're early."

"We didn't want to miss the amateur wrestling performance," Alexis said before introducing himself to Justin and me. Then Jeff jumped in and introduced us to Vadim. After shaking our hands, repeating our names twice each, committing them to memory, rating us on his threat index, Vadim turned to Jeff and tripped him with little effort. He then proceeded to instruct us in the art of street combat, demonstrating with pleasure on Jeff's body.

"You see," Vadim said while cranking Jeff's arm in a way the human arm was not meant to bend, "when you fight a man in real life it is not for sport. You think of the finish only. You ask one question of yourself. 'How do I ensure that this man before me may never challenge me again?' Then you answer this question through physical action. If you have the arm like this, you give all of your weight and snap it like wishbone."

"Oh cool. You guys do the wishbone in Russia?" I asked with genuine curiosity while Jeff screamed in pain. Vadim wasn't actually breaking Jeff's arm, but he was twisting it just enough to cause minor, albeit humorous, agony.

"Of course we have the wishbone," he answered, slowly releasing the tension from Jeff's arm while maneuvering to another hold. "What? You think we have a different chicken in Russia?" Without waiting for a response, he demonstrated a new move and showed various ways to inflict pain, broken bones, and unconsciousness from that position. Then he took a knife from his belt and pretended to stab Jeff in the neck, ribs, and finally a spot on the inside thigh where there was supposed to be a major artery. "For when you want slow, draining death that allows you to see life's truth in the eyes of your enemy as they transition from fear to acceptance, until the emotions reach zero, and the soul has left the body."

"Wow. I'd personally go with the quick neck-stab death. But I love the prose of the slow death," I said. Vadim finally got off of Jeff and helped him up, patting his head. Alexis and Justin were both laughing while Jeff fixed his hair and Vadim put his knife back in his belt.

"If you like the prose, you should read Dostoyevsky. You will learn of prose. Of life. Of death. Of all things that concern man."

"Oh, I've read Dostoyevsky," I blurted out, perhaps too enthusiastically. Vadim approached me until his eyes were within six inches of mine. I focused on the tip of his nose, knowing better than to look away but unable to deal with his intensity.

"You speak Russian?" He questioned, incredulously.

"Umm. No?"

"Then you have not read Dostoyevsky."

I had no interest in arguing so I just smiled.

"I've always preferred Tolstoy anyway," Alexis added as he stepped up to put his arm around my shoulder with one hand and Vadim's shoulder with the other, relieving the tension. "More of a working man's writer."

The five of us dined like kings on local street food and beer with ice in it. We talked like friends and had surprisingly mundane conversations about movies, music, and other trivial pop-culture topics. By the time we got to Aqua, the underground club of the aforementioned mob boss, it was packed. The host's booth had been reserved for us, and we were ushered immediately over to it, much to the dismay of several Parisian-types hoping the hundred Euros they were waving at the host would get them in ahead of us. Bottles of various liquors waited on glowing, decorative blocks. Beautiful women asked us what we'd like to drink and poured that for us before sitting in our laps to hand us our respective glasses. My designated girl had wide-set eyes and long legs, if a bit skinny for my taste. Looking around at the other girls, it seemed they were all versions of what Asian men thought white men would like. Though, judging from the interaction between my four comrades and their ladies, assumptions weren't far off. My lap girl took a shot of tequila and dribbled it into my mouth from hers.

Finally the man we had been waiting for appeared, surrounded by more lap girls and several African bodyguards. He knew how to make an entrance, that was for sure. The girl to his left carried an ashtray for his cigar. I didn't guess that he was the type to care about where he dropped his ash, so this was a clear affectation meant to impress. The girl to his right carried a golden chalice and a matching golden bottle of champagne. He took a drag of his cigar, a sip of his drink, handed both back to their respective holders, and then manufactured a large smile and extended his arms for hugs. The Russians first, of course, then Jeff. Justin, and I were introduced as creative consultants. He was very happy to have us as his guests, he assured us.

"I Max Rambo," he said. I tried not to but I must have made a question mark with my face. He explained, "This name not give me from Father. This name I choose. I choose all in life now. Now I boss."

"An excellent choice, in that case," I said, and I meant it. He was convinced of my sincerity and pleased with the compliment and motioned for us all to sit. Justin and I occupied ourselves while Jeff, the Russians, and Max Rambo discussed business.

After several more shots of tequila dribbled from my lap girl's mouth into my own, Max Rambo inserted himself next to me. "My friend, Paul. They say you creative chief, yes?"

"Umm. Yes, I guess that's true. My title anyway, is Chief Creative Officer."

"Chief. Creative. Officer." Max Rambo repeated it

back to himself slowly, deciding what it meant to him. "This the good title," he proclaimed. "You have many . . . ideas? Yes, Paul?"

"I suppose I do. My whole life, my job, everything I've done has been about ideas."

"Oh. Good. You have business card? I have need for very many ideas."

I handed him my card, and he examined it. Then he said something to one of his bodyguards, who walked off with purpose. I looked to Jeff, hoping nothing bad was about to happen. Jeff gave me the thumbs up. Then I thought I better get some assurances from a man of more stature and I turned to Vadim, who looked to me over the neck of his lap girl and gave me his own thumbs up before making a show of sticking it up the girl's skirt.

Max Rambo's bodyguard reappeared at our booth with a mermaid goddess. An Asian Jessica Alba. She wore tight superhero shorts and a fish-scaled bikini top. She stood before me, staring. I'm not sure, but my mouth might have dropped open.

"You like?" asked Max Rambo.

"She's amazing," I answered while she stood there like a rare breed of ox on display at a livestock auction.

"New girl. Best girl. Special menu. French man already reserve, but I cancel and offer you."

"Oh, that's so generous of you. What does 'special menu' mean, exactly? Because she's so hot?"

"Yes, this. Best girl. The virgin. One thousand US dollar, you fuck. Fifty thousand US dollar, you kill. Any way you want. My men clean after."

"What?" I had to make sure I heard him correctly.

"I say," he now screamed in my ear, "one thousand dollar, fuck. Fifty thousand dollar, make dead." I looked up at her. She did a poor job of hiding her anguish but made an honorable attempt at it. Despite her ethereal beauty, I wasn't sure that I was even interested in her. I didn't need any new complications in my life. But to say that I was not concerned for her as one human to another would be a lie. I looked back to Max Rambo as he continued, "Everything arrange. No problem. No," he searched for the words, "no jail. I have police agree."

"I've never heard of that before." I tried to hide my disgust and called on my facial musculature to create the closest representation of a poker face that I could generate. I asked him, "What if I want to keep her, but not kill her?" I approached it like a business negotiation, afraid that any betrayal of compassion would spoil my plan. I needed him to think I was simply bidding on a beast of burden that might be useful to my farming needs. "May I just buy her from you outright?"

He looked at me, into me. He was looking for something on which to anchor an opinion. "I don't know," he replied. "Bad business. But . . ." He seemed to be searching for an angle. "But, for new chief . . . creative . . . officer . . . for my business, *all* my business . . . is possible she is the gift." He smiled to see if I understood what he was saying.

"I would be open to making that deal with you," I said in a professional manner.

He put out his hand, and we shook in collusion. The blood, momentarily held in traffic by my internal tension, resumed its path through my circulatory system. He stood up and said something to one of his bodyguards. The bodyguard removed the girl who had been on my lap and placed Chan, as she was introduced, in her place. Then he said something to her in what I assumed was Cambodian. Her eyes widened as she took it in. Then she looked at me, studied me. She put her arms around my neck and let the side of her face fall into my chest and she held me like that for an awkwardly long time.

"The soft American," Vadim shouted to me, his voice punching its way through the thumping bass of the club, "this is what we will call our new friend." He held a glass half-full of something toward me in an air-toast. A hand from out of nowhere offered me a glass half-full of something that looked similar. I took it and air-toasted him in return, along with all of the others at the table.

Eventually, Chan lifted her head and stared into my eyes.

"You . . . like . . . me?" she asked, pointing toward her own chest to make sure I understood.

"Well, I don't want to kill you," I said and smiled. She gave a confused look and returned her face to my chest. Jeff took the opportunity to slide in by my side.

"Dude. I know you kind of like to go your own way, as the song says and all, but do you really think it's a good idea to fly home with another . . . another suitcase full of problems?"

"Trust me, dude," I assured him, "all of the above and more flashed through my head in the brief moments of the transaction. And it all happened quickly, I'll admit. But I had to. If I didn't kill her someone else would. And I wasn't gonna kill her."

"Noble enough. So, this is the adopt-a-bride chapter then?"

"No. I'll take her back and get her an apartment. Try to get her a job. I mean, worse comes to worst," now I spoke closer to him so she couldn't hear, "if worse comes to absolute worst, she can be a prostitute in Jakarta. But a normal one. She'll get major rupiah. High-class European clientele. And no one will ever pay to kill her."

Jeff considered it all and said, "Okay, homeboy. I respect it. I'll give her a job at the lounge then. She can be a cocktail girl or some shit."

I leaned back to look at Chan. I found it inconceivable that she achieved such a figure without the help of yoga or Pilates. Her eyes were not as preternaturally entrancing as Lusi's, no eyes would ever be, but her physique and facial features were on another level, which

I would never have imagined possible just a few hours prior. Had I met her months before, and had someone told me I had a shot in the world with her, I'd have been all in on superficial impressions alone. But by now, my skin had grown thick and less penetrable. I also had new priorities. Doing the right thing being priority one. Her salvation would be my own. I convinced myself of it.

Chan and I fell asleep only moments after touching my hotel bed. I awoke with her in my arms, but we never had sex.

"I owe my life you," she said slowly, word by word, hoping the syntax added up to mean what she wanted it to mean.

I half-expected the calls to prayer to punctuate her statement, but we were in the wrong country. Not sure what to say, I kissed her on the cheek and got up to shower. We spent the rest of the day by the pool with Jeff and Justin and the girls each of them had taken home from the club the night before. Vadim and Alexis came by as well, and we all had what some might consider a normal day, like normal people. Mimosas and other fruity cocktails, barbecued meats, water volleyball, and cannonballs. It could have been mistaken for a pool party in Cherry Hill, New Jersey. Pasadena, California. Hell, maybe Stonetown, Long Island. I relaxed on a lounge chair watching Chan and some of the other ladies drag Justin into the pool and pretend to drown him.

I wondered if she was someone my friend from the village might like to marry. I considered it for a while but concluded that he might not be equipped to take care of her. He couldn't give her the right life. Here was a girl who, under different circumstances, would be untouchable. In the streets of New York, she wouldn't have looked twice at me. At any guy I knew. She'd be unreachable, accessible only through the pages of swimsuit catalogs and fashion magazines. If I were lucky I'd have gotten the chance to say hi to her over the shoulders of her bodyguards in the green room of a late-late-night talk show. I didn't feel confident that my friend in the village could appreciate all of that.

But Chan was not beyond help. Nor was I.

PART 2

What you are about to read is not
written by Paul, but by me, Nisa,
who you surely know by now.
The "whys" and the "hows"
will all be explained.

CHAPTER 24

I didn't know that I was in love with Paul until after he fell in love with a prostitute. Befitting any proper tragedy, I didn't have a chance to tell him this until just before his death. I know that's a lot to hurl at you suddenly. Please, bear with me, and I will bring all to light.

I spent days in Paul's home after the news broke. Once the nature of events had become clarified, if not entirely clear, the local authorities decided there would no longer be a point to keeping officers posted there. I slept dreamless nights in the scent of Paul's bed and sometimes awoke in the dark and went out and swam naked in his pool. I don't remember exhaling once for several days. I wanted to take in and absorb every last drop of air that Paul had left behind, to wrap myself in what remained of his dissipating sense of being. I wasn't aware of what I was doing while doing it, but it felt like what I needed to do. It was the only thing that felt right because all in the world felt wrong to me. Friends asked how I could bare it, being there with such difficult memories. But Tetti was there during the days to distract me, and the most difficult memories were all at the office. I had not been in Paul's home since the day I first took him to see it.

It was the office, however, where I could not step foot, where trinkets of nostalgia hovered hauntingly like ghosts. It was there that I sat daily across a desk from him, or at times, together with him on his couch while we ate lunch, discussed and debated themes from books we were each reading or had read. Where we spoke about local cultural quirks and world events. It was in Paul's office, sitting on that couch, where my crossed leg would sometimes accidentally rub against his, where I'd see him look at my leg and look up at me and quickly distract himself from whatever he was thinking by offering a lame joke about something or other. It was in Paul's office where we'd teach one another small and subtle things about ourselves and our respective histories. Where one day I teased him as he brushed his growing, wavy hair out of his eyes that he was in danger of becoming a hippie and needed a haircut. It was in that office where he handed me the most thoughtful birthday present I'd ever been given, a black orchid, months after I had shared with him a story of how my grandparents used to take me hiking to find them in the hills outside of their home in Bukittinggi. It was in that office where we would listen to music on his fancy speakers. Where Paul taught me the little I now know about chess. Where I taught him the little he knew about Chinese checkers. Where we shared gossip. Where we discussed his friend in the village outside his window. Where we made plans for the creative department and where, day by day, more and more, Paul valued my input on his professional decisions. Paul's office was where he and I laughed together. Paul's office was where I fell in love with Paul.

Being in Paul's home, on the other hand, was pure fantasy. A place for me to create memories that never were, that I can only wish would have been. For seventy-two hours or so, I lived an illusion in the spartan cavern of a house in which Paul once existed without me. A place where Paul copulated with undeserving women. Where he awoke hungover on countless mornings to the sounds of prayer he knew nothing about. Where he spent unsober nights writing a novel that would one day be published and possibly sold for film rights. In Paul's home I sacrificed my jealousy and my ego and I allowed myself the most irrational of pleasures for three seemingly meaningless days that meant the world to me.

When I received word from his friends in NY that there would be a memorial service in his honor, I e-mailed Santi and the board of directors and told them I would not be returning to work again. I purchased a one-way ticket to JFK. I settled some affairs and I boarded a United Airlines flight, which, after a layover in Singapore, landed me in the marvelous city that never sleeps, just a few hours after my plane had taken off. It's a shame that Paul never had the opportunity to discover the magic of flying eastward across the international date line, through which time practically stands still. About two and a half hours after landing, my taxi was exiting the Long Island Expressway and I was rolling down my window to inhale the suburban scent of freshly cut lawns in Stonetown, where the people speak with heavy Italian accents, though few of them are Italian.

Two weeks after that, I was the proud tenant of a studio apartment in Greenpoint, Brooklyn, and ten months after that I was enrolled in the MFA program at the New School where I'm now completing my manuscript, the story of a heartbroken young Muslim girl from Indonesia who moves to a hip, secular community in New York City with the goal of writing the next great immigrant novel.

Recently, while procrastinating on my work, I reviewed for the first time since finding them in his house all of Paul's written pages and notes. I spent a weekend reading and rereading what he wrote. Once I started there was no stopping. A floodgate had opened, and I was riding the current to its conclusion. The first reading was like a punch in the throat. I won't bore you with details about all of the thoughts and feelings that choked me throughout. But it dug into me with great depth. More so, it entertained me. And I knew right away what I needed to do. I would fulfill the dream of Paul and complete his story.

Upon Lusi's return to Bali, something had changed in Paul. He attacked agency work with a new intensity, but he seemed distant and serious in a way that did not fit him. Then, after the Cambodia weekend he shifted yet again. He worked with the same drive but with a weightlessness that was contagious. The entire department felt new, and while the work continued to improve, it seemed more effortless than before, as if something had clicked. The staff was inspired and as an agency we were producing some of the best advertising in Southeast Asia. Many of the projects with which Paul was directly involved and some commercials that he directed himself went on to win international awards throughout Asia and Europe and even in the United States.

Paul and Santi developed a very powerful business relationship and won a large, new business pitch together, the billings from which transformed the agency overnight into a Goliath of a company. MBD had to add an entirely new floor of office space.

Despite these great financial successes for the agency and the board of directors initiating a new contract negotiation with a lucrative resigning bonus and other incentives in Paul's favor, Paul spoke much less of money. He spoke with excitement for the work itself. He gave agency-wide speeches on creativity for its own sake. He was asked to write a monthly column in the business section of a major Indonesian newspaper. He participated in a panel discussion at a local university and explained how religious leaders could employ creativity toward the purpose of peace and charity. This resulted in an invitation to the home of Shaikh Shamsi Tawhidi Bin Ali, a prominent Jakarta Imam. Paul was hesitant to accept until I explained to him how proud it would make the staff.

Paul joined a chess club and made a few local friends with whom he often spent time during weekends. He also continued to spend time with Jeff and Justin and was increasingly patient with Scotty, even though he still did not love Scotty. He also met with Chan once a week for coffee and he grew to love her like a sister.

It was a particularly busy week at the office when Paul received an e-mail from his client Indra inviting him to accompany him to Arena Club on the following Friday night.

"My wife and children have taken holiday back home in Mumbai," Indra explained to Paul in the e-mail, "and so it is only appropriate that the mice must play. We'll have a gentlemen's dinner and then an evening on the town, befitting the royalty of Babylon. L-O-L." He actually wrote the L-O-L like that.

And so it is here that our story resumes, another decadent night worthy of Paul's most gonzo tales. An adventure with this important client, Indra, who was not nearly the square that everyone who knew him guessed him to be. Of course, Paul would have had things no other way.

Arena Club represented its name well. It was like an indoor Roman coliseum converted to the cause of electronic dance music and the religion of sin. If there is a rock and roll heaven, then surely there must be a techno hell. Arena Club was that, minus the towering infernos. Servers were scantily clad vixens of the night with orthodontically implanted fangs. Paul had already been to dozens of grand nightclubs in his life. Expensive clubs. Decadent clubs. Clubs impossible to get into unless as the guest of a celebrity. Illegal clubs and any other type of club in the world that one could imagine. Not to mention that crazy club in Cambodia, owned by Max Rambo. And yet, Arena Club, at that moment in his life, took Paul to the darkest regressions of his heart and soul. He coped with that feeling the only way he knew how. He ordered a bottle of tequila and two shot glasses. Indra procured from a shadowy individual several doses of ecstasy, then ordered a bottle of Dom Perignon and two bottles of water, just in case.

"Do you ever enjoy cocaine, Paul?" Indra asked.

Paul coughed up some champagne. "Sorry. I wasn't expecting that."

"My apologies. I thought you to be a man of the world, Paul," Indra said with a laugh, a wink, and an endearing slap on Paul's knee.

"Well, I have been around," Paul said. "Don't get me wrong. I've definitely partied with colleagues and clients before. But you may be the first global-level client to bring up cocaine. And, to answer your question, I have enjoyed it here and there. I'm currently trying to change some things in my life though. Basically, all the clichés that people say after coming out the bright side of several wrong roads they don't wish to travel again." Then he added, with a devilish smile, "Plus, my new friend the Imam wouldn't really approve of cocaine."

"Of course, Paul," Indra joked, "he would surely only sign off on the liquor and MDMA. None of the hard stuff!" They both laughed heartily, and Indra changed the subject. "Aside from your newfound celebrity status within the local marketing community, you must be happy to have come full circle with your directing. It's what led you to advertising in the first place, is that right? And now you're directing again. The commercial you did for the Bank of Indonesia was a thing of beauty."

"It's funny how things work out," Paul said. "Originally, I thought I'd direct feature-length art films, but I was afraid there'd be no money in it. Or maybe I was just afraid, period. It's hard to say at this point. Commercials aren't exactly feature films, but when done right they really can be art. It's been more fulfilling than I expected."

"And you're still young, Paul, don't forget. You're smart to make your fortune now. Perhaps you'll make a great feature film in the future. You'll make your passion project. What would it be? Just for fun, tell me, Paul," Indra insisted.

"I'm thinking it'd be an adaptation of the novel I've been writing, which I was working on and then had to start over after all of my writing went missing in a house robbery. Something about an American advertising executive making his way in the Third World while coming to grips with an overall perspective shift, and of course, in the face of several unexpected challenges in life and love. He might also have all of his writing stolen in a house robbery. Sort of a pseudo-biopic romantic comedy with a heavy dose of international intrigue."

"You had mentioned working on the novel, but I didn't realize how serious you were," Indra said. "Should it become a movie, be sure to send me an invitation to the premiere, Paul."

"I'll do that." They toasted to it with shots and each took one more pill for good measure. "So, what about you, Indra? If you weren't a global marketing wizard, what would you be doing?"

"Thank you for asking, Paul," Indra replied. Then, after taking a drink from one of the several glasses of liquor now in front of him and directing a contemplative look out toward the crowd of hellions, "Since I was a very young child, I wanted to be an inventor. But I've always lacked a great idea and the ability to execute one successfully." At this he laughed so hard from the gut that he fell out of his seat. Two vixens lifted him back and one sat on his lap, anchoring him in place, and poured a shot across her chest for him to lick. Paul watched with pleasure as he laughed to himself. The scene felt dangerously familiar, but he couldn't stop his own laughter. He felt as if he were laughing for hours upon hours as the world around him revolved faster and faster and his sense of being began its slow, extended fade to black.

Shaking himself out of a forward head spin, lost in the deep frequencies of thrumming beats and electro-static sound waves, Paul forced his eyes open and his head up to realize he was hunched over himself on a deep green velvet couch, in a private room, somewhere in the bowels of the club. The cement walls were painted black, and a single fluorescent bulb, diffused by a translucent blue tarpaulin, hung overhead. On the floor in front of Paul was a lanky, nude, African woman stabbing a syringe into a vein in his foot, just between his big toe and the next. As she injected the substance into his body, Paul felt himself melt into the couch like butter on a warm dinner roll. His head drifted back against the soft fibers and flashes of incomprehensible visions played in his mind as his glazed green eyes rolled in his head and he weaved in and out of existence.

Paul found his way to consciousness once more and was overcome with relief to find himself wrapped in the sheets of his own bed, albeit with no idea how he'd gotten there or where his clothes were. It was still dark outside. When he heard the morning's first calls to prayer singing to him through the window, he felt an unexpected sense of comfort and involuntarily muttered

ROBERT P. COHEN

to himself, "Inshallah." He tried to stand and felt an im-
mense pressure against his skull, causing him to collapse
upon the hard, ceramic floor. Despite the head trauma,
the cold tile felt like relief. He pressed his face against it,
one cheek at a time. The rest of his body slowly awoke
as he started feeling new pains and sensations. Random
aches announced their occupancy throughout his me-
ridian. When he realized there was pain coming from
his penis he looked toward his crotch to find a torn condom had somehow wrapped itself around his shaft like a
tourniquet. Dried blood and vomit were crusted around
his chest and stomach and pelvic area and down his leg.
Broken to the core, he curled himself into fetal position
as the prayers wafted through the room and entered his
DNA with each laboring breath.

When he opened his eyes next, morning light was
breaking through the window shades. Chan was helping
him up from the floor and guiding him to an already
drawn bath. He was confused about her presence but
felt a great contentment in it. She held his penis, care-
fully removed the broken condom, and fought the urge
to shake her head judgingly at him. A single, silent tear
dripped from her face. He couldn't look her in the eyes.
His throat was in flames and his stomach was playing
games with gravity. Chan brushed his hair with her long,
narrow fingers and his head drifted back until it rested
on the tub's smooth porcelain edge. He let his eyelids
close but did not fall back asleep. She washed his body

like a mother bathing her sick child. Neither had uttered a word to the other until she kissed his forehead and said, "Relax. I make coffee, come back soon."

"How did you . . . what are you doing here?" Paul finally asked.

"Tetti find you on floor and call Nisa. Nisa call me to come," she said. "Don't worry. I go kitchen and be back soon."

"Your English is getting better," Paul whispered.

She smiled and said, "I be back." But she said it like the Terminator, which she had recently seen on her new television, and Paul wanted to smile but his body ached too greatly to do so.

Paul drank his coffee and stared at the ceiling while Chan sat on the edge of the tub watching Japanimation episodes on her iPhone, which Paul had bought for her the week prior. She wore headphones so she wouldn't disturb him and every now and then she let out an audible giggle and covered her mouth with her hand.

Later, Chan sliced some fruit and made more coffee. She toasted some wheat bread and buttered it and brought it all for Paul to eat in his bed.

"I don't think I've ever felt like this in my life," he said.

"I not ask what you do. When I come, you look so bad. Like the dead man, but alive. Almost not alive," she said.

"I don't even remember, Chan. Why was Tetti here today?" he asked.

"She no work today?" Chan replied.

"She has off on Sundays."

"But Monday today."

"What? How is that possible?"

"Monday today. Or, today Monday, is better?"

"Today is Monday," Paul offered. "But, I went to the club Friday night. There's no way. Even if I partied all night, came home late Saturday, slept until Sunday . . . Where did Sunday go? I didn't even fly across the international dateline."

"Where you fly?"

"Oh, no, I didn't fly. Long story. But Monday?"

"Today is Monday," Chan said with confidence.

"Wow."

"I say it right?"

"Yes. Great job," Paul said. "You're a good friend, Chan."

"Eat more."

Once Paul regained his wits and seemed mostly self-sufficient, Chan left him and said that she'd call later.

Paul checked his phone, which Chan had been kind enough to plug in and charge for him at some point during her visit. It was indeed Monday. Now 12:28 p.m. There were thirty-two unread text messages waiting for him.

#1, Saturday, 2:53 a.m., Indra: Where are you Paul? Looking around but can't seem to find you.

#2, Saturday, 2:58 a.m., Indra: There are Japanese tourists dancing on the seats where we were sitting. No idea where you are. Please reply.

#3, Saturday, 3:24 a.m., Indra: Please reply, Paul. Not sure how long I can stand to be here. I'll look for you a little while longer.

#4, Saturday, 4:41 a.m., Indra: Just caught glimpse of you on other side of club. Two Africans! Looks promising. Please forgive me but I'm on verge of collapse. I'll send my driver back for you shortly. Check in when able. I hope you have condoms.

#5, Saturday, 9:47 a.m., Nisa: How was your night with Indra? I hope you men didn't get into too much trouble ;-P

#6, Saturday, 1:17 p.m., Suri: Hello Paul. Do you come to chess club today? We start already but hope to see you here. Inshallah

#7, Saturday, 3:33 p.m., Santi: Hello, Mr Chief Creative Officer. My beautiful, single cousin is ready to meet you. She could make very good wife, lol ☺ ☺

Maybe I have you both to our house for bbq next weekend? Exciting? Let me know, please.

#8, Saturday, 4:21 p.m., Jeff: What up homeboy! It's 420! Scored some primo ganja from some dutch pals in town. My house tonight. Bongs n beer. Some of the boys and a few ladies coming through. Nothing crazy though. Don't worry. See ya round 7.

#9, Saturday, 4:48 p.m., Indra: Paul, just woke up on raft in my pool. Unsure how I landed there. So unsafe. Going to bed now but concerned no word from you. My driver is waiting on same corner where he dropped us. If you can't find him here is his contact: 021-30289888

#10, Saturday, 5:15 p.m., Chan: I go Jeff house party. You go? See you there? I have news I tell you.

#11, Saturday, 5:52 p.m., Justin: Mate! How goes it? Heading to Jeff's? Gimme a call if can. Wanna talk to you about something beforehand.

#12, Saturday, 8:44 p.m., Jeff: Hey boss you coming? Totally chill crew here. Good times. Get your ass over!

#13, Saturday, 9:50 p.m., Chan: Why you no come?

#14, Sunday, 12:35 a.m., Justin: Mate. Hope all's okay. Everyone's been asking for you. Give a shout tomorrow we'll grab coffee and catch up.

#15, Sunday, 9:26 a.m., Indra: Paul! Woke to a text from my driver. Sounds harrowing! Glad he found you and remembered your home. Call me when you wake if you're able. Based on my hangover I imagine yours will rival Hiroshima! Good luck!

#16, Sunday, 10:00 a.m., Nisa: Are you alive? Busy? Just checking.

#17, Sunday, 10:12 a.m., Jeff: Dude. Wake n bake with the dutchies? Brunch? Let's do it.

#18, Sunday, 10:24 a.m., Purwoko: Morning boss. Sorry to bother you on weekend. We had idea to share. If you have time, please check email. Thank you.

#19, Sunday, 11:36 a.m., Jeff: Okay, whatever you're up to must be good. Last text, but did I mention one of my pals has two sisters with him. Tall. Blond. Dutch! Probably won't go for you but fun to look at in bikinis. We're by the pool. Plus Justin and Chan are here. I'm high but I might have seen them kiss?

#20, Sunday, 12:56 p.m., Nisa: Sorry to bother you,

Paul. Some of the teams have work for you to look at if you don't mind. They've worked the weekend. There's a meeting tomorrow. Please try to check and reply.

#21, Sunday, 3:15 p.m., Indra: Paul. Hope you are rested by now. Wife and children arriving home any minute. Lord save me!

#22, Sunday, 4:21 p.m., Jeff: 4:20. Had to say it.

#23, Sunday, 5:02 p.m., Nisa: Chan called to ask if I knew where you are. Do I need to be worried? Aside from the work and the teams, I hope you're okay. Please call or write.

#24, Sunday, 6:27 p.m., Justin: Hey Mate. You off on some exotic escapade? At least send pics.

#25, Sunday, 8:30 p.m., Indra: Rough day, my friend. Made it through though. Just put the kids down to sleep. Got a reminder from my secretary that "the agency" will be presenting new campaign ideas for the acne creams tomorrow. Would you be angry if I skipped? Hahaha. I joke. I suppose if I don't hear from you prior I'll see you there. See if we can keep straight faces!

#26, Sunday, 10:42 p.m., Max Rambo: My chief of creative. 500 yrs I no hear you. Call soon. We work.

You come here help me with idea. Stay my home. Many women. Many drink. Very fun. Work and play. Call now.

#27, Monday, 6:42 a.m., Chan: I come now.

#28, Monday, 6:43 a.m., Nisa: Paul! If you get this . . . Tetti found you on floor. Sent me picture of you! OMG! Don't be mad. She's worried. Don't think appropriate if I come. I called Chan. She's on her way. I hope you're okay!

#29, Monday, 6:44 a.m., Nisa: Don't worry, btw. I deleted photo and told Tetti to do same.

#30, Monday, 8:35 a.m., Nisa: Chan texted to say you're in bad shape but bathing. I hope you'll be okay. I know you won't be able to check this yet but check in when can. I have some questions about work-related matters for the day. On way to office now. I'll handle all until I hear from you.

#31, Monday, 10:48 a.m., Santi: I stopped by your office to discuss some things. Nisa tells me you're not feeling well. I hope you'll be able to make the meeting today. Is it okay if the team shows me the work without you if not? I know it will be great but I must prepare my presentation. Of course I'm also curious to hear from you about the other matter!

#32, Monday, 11:51 a.m., Nisa: Sorry to bother you so much. The board of directors are asking about you. I told them you're not feeling well. Also Santi stopped by. I hope it's okay I'm going to have the team show her the work.

Paul took a moment to absorb it all and tapped my name on his phone. I answered on the first ring, "Paul! You called. Finally. How are you?"

"I've been better." He sounded drained of life.

"I'm glad to hear your voice. Sorry about all the texts. I was worried. And there's so much going on. I'm doing my best to handle things. Everyone is looking for you. The teams. The account people. The board of directors. I'm guessing you won't be coming in?"

"I don't know. Maybe I should. What time is the acne presentation?"

"Four in the afternoon," I said.

"Not four in the morning?" he croaked.

"I'm glad your sarcasm is alive and well."

"It'll be the last part of me to die. Have you seen the work?" he asked.

"The team did show me. Is that okay?"

"Of course. How was it?"

"One campaign, it's maybe too smart," I said with a question mark, unsure of whether or not he'd take my criticism of ad work seriously. "There are some clever headlines but I wonder, maybe it'll be too much to think about for the audience. Does that make sense?"

"Yes. What about the rest?" he asked without the need for elaboration.

"Well there is only one other option. But I like that one," I said. "It's very cute and playful. It makes me feel like having the acne is not a big deal. Like it's a fact of life that we've all dealt with and it's easy to fix with this product. Some exciting online, interactive elements for consumers to engage with as well."

"Did Santi like it?" he asked.

"They're showing her now."

"Okay, but you like it?"

"Yes. The second one I like very much, actually." I was excited that he was so interested in my thoughts. I assumed it was due to the state he was in. But it made me feel good to have him value my opinion in this way. To feel like he could rest assured in his weakened state that he had me to rely on.

"That's cool. They only need to buy one idea. I have a feeling Indra won't want to waste a minute more than he needs to today. As long as he likes the one option, we're good. Maybe I should go."

"Have you spoken to him? To Indra?" I asked.

"Not yet. I had a few texts from him though."

"Paul, should I even ask what went on?"

"Probably not. Maybe one day. I know I said before I'm done with that kind of life but I'm really done now. Finished. Done. Seriously. Should I go to the meeting?"

"Paul, honestly, you don't sound very . . . present-able." I was being kind. He sounded like a man on his deathbed.

"Maybe I should go," he insisted.

"Okay. I'll tell Rahim. He's at your house, by the way."

"What? Where?"

"I imagine he's waiting by the car," I said.

"Oh, shit. I'll go let him in. What about the board of directors?"

"Definitely do not contact them today. I will hold them off and schedule you a meeting with them for tomorrow."

"Good thinking."

"That's what I'm here for," I said with a smile and an internal wink.

"Wanna hear some crazy shit?"

"I'd love to."

"Santi texted me yesterday. Talking again about set-ting me up with her cousin."

I laughed out loud, more a nervous reaction than anything. "How odd," I said.

"Isn't it? But I have to admit, I wonder if I should go for it. Maybe I really need to settle down already. Live clean. Exercise more. Take up yoga. Wheatgrass. Get married. Have kids. White picket fence and all. The book'll turn out less exciting, but . . . are there any white picket fences in Jakarta? I don't think I've seen any."

"Umm. Wow. That's a lot to decide now. Maybe you should . . ." I was such a coward. But what was I going to say at a time like this?

CHAPTER 25

Paul swung the thick, golden Garuda knocker against the large oak door, expecting a maid to answer, but when the door opened it was Santi standing there. She smiled with the spark of a long lost relative, reunited after many years.

"Well, hello Paul!" she exclaimed, as if surprised to see him. "Everyone is in the courtyard now. They're all excited for your arrival, our guest of honor." She held out the "honor" in an affected way. Paul's reaction was to be confused, but he made a conscious effort to be positive. He smiled back at her and handed her a bottle of Pappy Van Winkle, twenty-year reserve. He had debated before his visit over whether to save that bottle for himself and bring a cheaper liquor. In the end, he felt that putting his best foot forward would be the best plan.

"A peace offering," Paul said.

"You're too kind. Too kind. You didn't need to," Santi said. "But," she continued, "I better hide it in the study. Don't want to offend the very Muslim guests here."

"Oh, right!" Paul said. "I thought you were . . . I'm sorry, I didn't think . . ."

"Don't worry, Paul. Richard and I do drink. But we have more conservative guests here and it will be best not to wave it in front of them all."

"Understood."

"Best to watch the language too," she said with a playful smirk.

Paul resisted the urge to respond with a sarcastic string of the foulest language he could conjure. He settled on basic sarcasm in the form of a humble brag, "But the Imam enjoyed my cursing." Santi chuckled silently and Paul was at least 50 percent confident that she knew he was joking.

Santi handed the bottle to a maid, instructing her where to take it, then led Paul through a formidable hallway toward the courtyard. The house was a mansion by any standards. Crystal chandeliers crowded a path across the ceiling, and their luminance bounced in speckled flurries off of the ornate, gold-flecked wallpaper. Two pit bulls approached to sniff Paul's crotch, and he patted their heads.

"Don't mind them. They're big babies. They love men, as you can tell," she said.

Through a large entranceway they walked out to a patio where there were far more people than Paul was expecting, including half a dozen gentlemen adorned in full military uniforms. Paul did his best to convey a good energy as the crowd turned to take him in.

"Everybody," Santi announced, "this is Mr. Paul

Goldberg, the chief creative officer at MBD advertising. He's very smart and funny, and we're happy to have him with us." The crowd clapped and bellowed various greetings at him. He smiled, fake and wide, and waved to individuals in the directions of the respective greetings and murmurs that he heard. Santi led him toward the grill, where many of the military men congregated.

He was introduced to several characters of high-ranking titles, including one general, who turned out to be Santi's father-in-law. This was a man who was widely, if silently, known to be responsible for an untold number of political executions. He was famous during the communist massacres for teaching the anti-communist thugs cost-effective ways of mass slaughter, one of which involved strangling by steel wire, which also lacerated the necks of the victims so that they would simultaneously bleed out while being choked. It was a messy ordeal but it helped to conserve bullets and worked toward the government's PR efforts to dissuade those who might wish to join the resistance. In more recent times, this general was known, through paranoid whispers, for his unique take on democracy, which was based on the theory that if opposition candidates dropped out of a race due to a death in the family, or their own death, there would be no need to tamper with any votes.

The general's son, Santi's husband, Richard, named for an American ex-president who aided the current party's rise to power and said general's place in history, was manipulating slabs of various meats on the grill. After some words with the general, during which Paul decided not to explore his hunch that these men were probably familiar with Vadim, Alexis, and possibly Max Rambo, Richard turned from his piles of charring flesh to greet Paul. They shook hands like men with a past, and it lasted several seconds longer than what might be considered normal. But when they pulled away from each other's grasp they each accepted the situation for what it was and had a mutual, unspoken understanding that they would remain on this path of civility.

"Breaking bread, Paul," Richard began, for the benefit of those within earshot, "is a way of bonding, older than both of our people. World peace has been brokered over lesser feasts than what we will share today. I welcome you to my home and hope that you will find happiness here in my country."

"Thank you, Richard. Really. That means a lot to me," Paul said, unsure if it actually meant a lot to him, resisting the urge to criticize Richard's rhetoric, even if silently in his own mind.

"Richard," Santi broke in, "Paul brought something very special for you. It is in the study now."

"Actually," Paul said quietly to Richard so that no one else could hear, "it's a nice, rare bourbon. Pretty hard to get. But I have a friend who knows a guy."

"I would like the names and addresses of your friend and this guy," the general said. Apparently, he was closer than Paul had realized. Or possessed preternatural hearing abilities. Paul turned with concern, wondering if he'd just incriminated himself and several others in one breath. Then the general burst into laughter. "I joke with you, Paul! We are men of the real world here." He slapped Paul on the back. Richard and Santi laughed sincerely with the general. Paul laughed a forced laugh because he didn't know how else to respond.

"Paul, let us visit my study to talk more privately," Richard said, handing the meat tongs to a man beside him. He led the way as they walked toward the house. It was a slow walk as Richard was greeted by many guests along the way and felt the need to introduce Paul to each of them. Some of them knew who Paul was or had heard of him and asked several questions, not limited to whether or not he was married or had a girlfriend and if he was lying. By the time they reached the bar in the study, Paul had met some of the most corrupt military men, politicians, business tycoons, and religious figures in Indonesia. He also came across two of his bank clients and was forced to make small talk about consumer trends and film production for several minutes before Richard politely pulled him away. For that, Paul was most grateful.

"You don't like talking to clients very much, do you Paul?" Richard asked.

"I like talking to some more than others. Mostly, I was just hoping to keep things casual and unprofessional today. But we all play the game, right?"

"You seem very good at this game. But for some reason, I sensed that you did not want to talk to them. Or I would have left you to your business," Richard said.

"Oh. I hope they couldn't tell," Paul said with a smile. "But it just caught me off guard. Wrong venue."

"I understand. And no, they could not tell. I am sure of it. But I have a particularly developed instinct for reading people. It is what makes me so good at what I do. Just like you have certain instincts that make you good at what you do, correct?"

"Yes, you're right," Paul said, choosing not to ask Richard any specifics about what exactly it was that he did.

"I've heard very good things about your talents, Paul," Richard said.

"Oh, from Santi? That's nice of her."

"Well, yes. Santi says very good things. That there is a new understanding between you both, and that business has never been better. That makes me pleased to hear. But I have heard positive word from others in Jakarta as well. Mr. Indra, for instance."

"Our client, Indra? I didn't know you knew him."

"Yes. He has been a very important client for Santi for many years. We break bread often. Maybe once every third or fourth month. My father and I have helped his company as well. It is not always easy to get approvals for certain new product imports without friends in the right places. I suppose we are the guy he knows. Right, Paul?"

"Indeed," Paul agreed politely.

Richard dropped two ice cubes each in two glasses and then poured some of the Pappy Van Winkle.

"Cheers, Paul," Richard said. "Tonight, we will enjoy the offerings of life and break bread and be merry. Drink up. Let us have one more glass before we venture out to the crowds and to your meeting with the cousin of Santi."

They each finished their drink quickly before Richard poured another round.

Paul was fascinated by Richard's English. It was nothing like what he expected based on the texts and conversation he had with Richard months prior. Had Richard been putting on a goon-like demeanor for effect? What an interesting man, he thought. Paul couldn't help but wonder what other quirky methods Richard employed against his enemies. He was also amazed at Richard's ability to speak without using a single conjunction.

"Paul, would you like to meet Cindy now?"

"Who?"

"Cindy. The cousin of Santi."

"Oh, right. The whole reason I'm here. Well, sure. I hope it's not too built up. But hey, let's do it." He finished his drink, and Richard placed both of their glasses on a gold-plated tray.

With a great sense of positivity and a comfortable layer of buzz, Paul followed Richard back out to the courtyard and found Santi with a group of other women. When Paul and Richard reached the group Santi beamed with excitement as the rest of the gaggle giggled like children.

"Paul!" Santi shouted. "Please. You must meet my cousin, Miss Cindy." Santi pulled him by the arm until he was awkwardly close to Cindy, who appeared ready to burst from shyness. Paul felt a sandbag in his stomach and hoped beyond hope that his reaction was not washing over his manufactured smile. Cindy was not the ugliest girl he had ever seen, but, to be polite, she was far from attractive. She wore a dress that was too tight for her body. In fact, she might not have appeared as out of shape as she did, because technically, she was only slightly overweight, if only she had worn something that fit her better. Her makeup was plastered on, as if a little girl had gotten into her mother's beauty supplies for the first time. Her hair was reminiscent of a 1980s American infomercial, and her teeth were so bad they could have offended a Manchester junkie. Her smile was the second worst that Paul had seen during his time in Indonesia, and therefore, ever. Strangely, she resembled Santi to a degree. But Santi, who was fair to slightly above average, superficially speaking, appeared as a goddess next to Cindy. What's worse, the amount of gold and jewels adorning Cindy from head to toe betrayed a materialistic aesthetic that reminded Paul of his own worst, former qualities, some of the very qualities he was hoping to leave in his past. Paul began writing scripts in his mind, editing and rehearsing them before he let any words leave his mouth, wanting to be absolutely sure that at no point in the approaching conversation would anything stupid or life-threatening be said.

"It's so nice to meet you, Cindy," Paul said. All of the girls giggled.

"Very nice to meet you, Paul," Cindy said. The girls giggled again. Paul wondered if this was all a test of some sort. How could Santi have thought that Paul would be attracted to this woman?

"So, Cindy, do you live near here as well?" Paul asked. The girls all giggled, yet again.

"Well, well, well, Paul," Santi interjected. "Trying to go home with her already? Slow down, Mr. Cowboy!" She laughed loudly at herself, as did everyone except for Paul and Cindy.

"Stop it, please, Santi," Cindy pleaded with her cousin. Then she said to Paul, "I just moved back to town and I do live somewhat close. Only two kilometers from here."

"Oh, so just like an hour or two from here?" Paul joked. Nobody laughed.

"No, Paul. Two kilometers is not very far at all," Cindy reasoned. "A little over a mile for you, no? Very close."

"I was just joking. Because of the traffic and, you know, Jakarta," Paul said.

"Yes. There is very much traffic in Jakarta, Paul," Cindy said.

They continued with this awkward conversation for some time until Santi's mother summoned her and Cindy to help with some domestic duties. Paul and Cindy promised to find one another later, after the feast. Richard asked Paul back to the study for bourbon refills and Paul was awash with relief to see the predicament come to a temporary end.

CHAPTER 26

On the same night as the barbecue at Santi's house, I had Chan as a guest in my own home, for tea and confession.

"Chan, can you promise me to keep a secret?" I asked.

"Of course, Nisa. You are my friend. I promise you to keep the secret. Is correct way I say?"

"Yes, Chan. And thank you. But, before I tell you, can I ask you something else?"

"Yes. It is okay. What will you ask me, Nisa?" Her English really was improving.

"You don't have feelings for Paul, do you?" I asked.

"Feelings for Paul? It means, do I care for him?"

"Well, more than care for him. A friend can care for him. I'm asking if you love him. If you want him as your lover?"

"No, Nisa. I tell you that I with Justin now. You remember?" she reminded me, making me feel like a silly little girl.

"Yes, of course. I know that. But sometimes people are with someone and care about someone else. I don't mean to suggest anything, I'm just nervous," I explained.

"I care for Paul because he is my great friend now.

Understand? The best friend. And I care for Justin with love like the lover for sex. And he in my heart now. I say it correctly?"

"Yes, Chan. You say it beautifully."

"What will you tell me?" Chan asked.

"I think I'm in love with Paul," I said with trepidation. "Is that horrible?"

"Not horrible," Chan said reassuringly, reaching over to grab my hand. "This is the good news, Nisa. I am sure he has the same love for you."

"You think he does? He told you that?" I asked anxiously.

"He never tells me that. I guess it but I never say. I guess about you and I guess about him. Sure I'm right. I am sure."

"I hope so. I don't know. He's always interested in such exotic women, like you."

"But Paul is not interested with me. You know. And you are very pretty. He did tell me you have the cute dimples."

"He said that?"

"Yes. Something he say . . . no . . . said, about the dimples and . . . to eat the cereal, like breakfast, from your dimples, yes. I don't understand but he tell me it is very good," she said. I laughed and thought about what kind of odd metaphor Paul could have been using to compare my dimples to cereal. But in that moment, I felt giddy and thought there could be a real chance.

Chan and I drank a bottle of rice wine and gossiped through the night. We talked about Paul, of course. We talked about Justin, who turned out to be more of a romantic than I would have guessed. We talked about all of the boys and took turns listing the top five Hollywood celebrities with whom we would like to have sex. Then Chan told me that I should call Paul and tell him how I felt. That's when I remembered where he was.

"But he's with Santi now. Meeting her cousin. They are being introduced as possible love interests. He'll probably marry her!" I was irrationally frantic.

"Nisa, you know Paul. He know you. You are best for him. I see this."

"But does he think so, too? I wish he'd give me a sign."

"But, Nisa," she said, "he is the man." Then, after a subtle pause, proving her newfound understanding of Western comedic timing, "Stupid." We both fell on the floor laughing. I reached up to the coffee table for my phone and called Paul but he didn't answer.

CHAPTER 27

"So, tell me, Paul," Richard said while pouring drinks, "how did you feel while talking to Cindy? I imagine the situation was very tense for you, yes?"

"I can't say it wasn't a little bit awkward," Paul replied.

"Yes. Santi can be aggressive with such things. But she loves her cousin and wants her with a good man. You are a good man, Paul, are you not?"

"I like to believe I am. But, you know, chemistry is a funny thing," Paul said.

"The chemistry between you and Cindy?" Richard questioned.

"Well, I wanted to be polite," Paul explained. "And I appreciate Santi's efforts. Really, I do. But I'm not so sure about me and Cindy"

"Is that so? Many men would feel lucky to be introduced to Cindy," Richard fired back, incredulous. "A woman from a good family. A relative by law of a very important family, as well. Does she not suit you, Paul?"

"To be honest, she's not exactly my type," Paul admitted.

"And what exactly is your type, Paul?" Richard seemed to be annoyed now.

"Well, being attractive, for one." As soon as Paul said this, he wished he hadn't.

"Excuse me? You do not find Cindy to be attractive?" Richard measured.

"Well, she might be. Just not the type that I'd usually go for," Paul tried to negotiate his way back to polite conversation.

"Again, Paul, with your type. It is said that Cindy is similar to Santi. Is Santi not attractive according to your 'type'?" Richard's voice was rising in volume.

"This feels like a trick question," Paul said and finished the rest of his drink. He picked up the bottle and took the liberty of pouring himself one more round, no ice.

"There are no tricks here, Paul. I am merely examining the facts of the matter." Richard held out his glass for Paul to fill. "What is your opinion of Santi? Superficially speaking."

"She's pretty?"

"You don't seem sure of yourself, Paul."

"I'm not really sure where you want this conversation to go."

"I am simply attempting to manifest some clarity here, Paul. You are a guest in my home. My beautiful wife has invited you, against my better judgment, to make a match between her cousin and yourself, also against my better judgment. You come here, you seem to be, or at least act as if you are, more of a gentleman than I had given you credit for being. Now I am forced to feel the fool for believing such deception as you sit here and insult these beautiful women. My wife. My cousin by law."

"I didn't insult anyone. You asked me and I told you. They're just not my type. I'm into different kinds of women. More exotic women, I guess," Paul said, attempting to negotiate a delicate path. He tried to hold back his true thoughts but failed entirely when he said, "I just don't like large, gaudy women, for fuck's sake."

As he was flying backward through the air, Paul thought to himself all of the better ways he could have said what he said. Just as his glutes, and then his back, and then his head made contact with the rug, he realized that anything short of declaring his love for Cindy would most likely have produced a similar, hostile response from Richard. It was built into the situation. It was the logical outcome of the plot. And so too was Paul's decision finally to fight, swinging a wild leg upward toward a charging Richard. As Richard's right foot made contact with Paul's rib cage, the forward motion of Paul's swinging leg swept Richard's left foot out from under him, causing Richard to lose his balance and fall toward and through the antique glass coffee table behind them. It was a crash so violent in its tone that Paul felt it had to have been heard around the world. Due to the build and size of the house, it was barely even noticed by the maids down the hall, let alone any of the relatives and guests outside in the yard with their boisterous conversations and light jazz playing through patio speakers.

Paul rolled to his knees and reached out to peel Richard off of the brass frame that once held, as one solid piece, the glass sections that now punctured Richard. Shards stuck like crystal formations from several places in Richard's body. His stomach. His chest. His neck. His face. A puddle of dark red rippled across the golden carpet on which he now lay. Richard grasped weakly at his wounds, instinctively attempting to prioritize which needed tending most. He pulled curiously at a shard in his neck and blood sprayed the room around him.

Paul stood silent as he observed the scene from outside of himself. He felt the dread that he knew was supposed to be there all along finally wash over him. Paul wondered what Richard would have done had the situation been reversed.

As the blood pouring from the wounds in Richard's body slowed to a drip, Paul felt his own body temperature plunge. He looked over to see the bottle of bourbon they'd been drinking, still half-full. He took it in his hand, looked down at Richard once more, and he ran.

CHAPTER 28

"Nisa," Paul said when I answered the phone. Then he said nothing.

"Paul, is everything okay? How was the barbecue?" I asked, innocently.

"Nisa, something bad happened," he said.

"What happened, Paul? Where are you?" There were loud, industrial sounds in the background.

"I'm at the marina. Jeff arranged a boat. To get me out," Paul said, mechanically.

"A boat?" I was so confused. "To get out? Get out of what? What's going on, Paul?"

"It was an accident, Nisa. Santi's husband, Richard. He's dead. I did it, I think. But it was an accident."

"What? Paul, are you joking? Please tell me it's a joke." I prayed that it would be a joke.

"We were arguing. I didn't like Cindy. I might have insulted Santi. I might have said 'the fuck' too. I'm not sure. He attacked me. I kicked him. In defense. Into a glass table. The table stabbed him."

"Oh, Paul. This sounds like one of your crazy ideas. Please tell me it's a joke," I begged.

"It's not a joke, Nisa. I'm in trouble, and I have to leave. Talk to Jeff when we get off. But I wanted to call you myself."

"But Paul . . ."

"What, Nisa?" he said, softly now. I could hear him fighting back tears.

"I want to see you, Paul," I blurted. "I need to see you."

"Oh Nisa. I wish I could see you, too. But I think I have to go right away. I'm really sorry. About everything. I should have been smarter. I never should have gone tonight. You should have told me not to," he reasoned.

"Paul, how could I . . ." I didn't even know what to say then.

"I'm not . . . you couldn't have. You didn't have to. I just. I have to get out of here. They're waving me on now. I can't believe this, Nisa."

"Where will you go? How will I speak to you? Or know anything?"

"We'll meet next year, in Paris," he said, trying to laugh his way through his sobs.

"Think of what a perfect ending to the book that will be," I said.

"You're amazing, Nisa. You're unbelievably amazing and I'm a total idiot. I'll talk to you soon. I promise."

After we hung up I kneeled on my floor and, for the first time in a very long time, I pleaded with my God.

CHAPTER 29

As I found out from Jeff, days after the fact, Paul had Rahim drop him off at the airport, where he took a taxi back to town and then another one from there to the marina. It wasn't that they didn't trust Rahim. They just didn't want to put him in a difficult position when questioned. Paul even walked into the airport before walking out again, hoping he would be captured on at least one surveillance camera to corroborate what would be Rahim's story.

Jeff arranged a deal involving a smuggler with whom he often did business. The man had a boat leaving the next morning to Hong Kong. Jeff convinced the man, with the help of a five-thousand-dollar bribe, to leave immediately and with one new addition of a human who was not to be listed on the ship's manifest. The thinking was that Paul could get on the next plane from Hong Kong to America. Jeff joked, maybe to cheer me up, "But knowing that dude, he might have made his way to Max Rambo in Cambodia, for more material."

"Jeff, he had enough material before he ever landed in Indonesia. That beautiful fool," I said.

"This is true, Nisa. But he never would have met us. We never would have met him."

"This too is true, Jeff," I said as we hugged one another as if we were each hugging Paul.

I like to think that as Paul sat there on his sea voyage, allowing thoughts to flow in and out of his mind like the tide, at least some of those thoughts were about me. The selfish person within me wishes that he realized he felt the same way that I did. That he had regrets about not being with me. That he yearned for all of the things that might be different had he been with me instead of at that house with Santi and her husband. He could have been in my bed. The two of us, making love like a man and woman who would one day become husband and wife.

In reality, I think Paul thought mostly of what would happen to his friend in the village next to the office. Paul wondered how he could get word to me to get his money to the man. He wondered how the man would spend that money. Would he buy a house? Would he help the kids or others in the village, or would he just leave his old world behind? Would he buy a motorbike? Would he buy nice clothes and get a job? Or would he spend all of the money on food and liquor? Drugs? Would he go to Arena Club and host a gang of prostitutes and take them each back to a private room one at a time, draining himself of a lifetime of sexual wanting?

I think Paul would have thought of his staff. Wondered if they would stay motivated. If they would continue the hard work in which they had only just begun to build momentum. He'd wonder if they would think of him fondly. Would they remember having learned anything at all from him? Or would they see him as the man who murdered a fellow Indonesian from an important, if questionable, family? A fellow Muslim.

He definitely thought of his friends Justin and Chan. Would they marry? Would they have children? Would he ever see them again?

He thought of Vadim and Alexis and Max Rambo and wondered how they'd feel about what had happened. Would Vadim be proud of him? Would he critique his technique? Would he be the only one who believed it was an accident, knowing deeply that Paul did not have it in him to kill? Would Max Rambo care, one way or the other? Or would he only be mad to have lost his chief of creative? Would he try to reclaim Chan if the contract had been breached? "No," Paul would have thought, "I'll have to work out some remote deal with Mr. Rambo. We'll work by phone and e-mail. Or he'll need to fly me in on a private jet and provide personal security."

He thought of his friends in New York. He wondered if the Stonetown crew would have finally applauded him for "representing." For standing strong in a fight, despite his victory being only from luck, if one wanted to call it that. He thought of his friends in the advertising industry, who would tell such well-crafted anecdotes of his adventures to their friends at wrap parties in Los Angeles and industry events in France.

I'm sure he thought of many things in that dark world in which he found himself. But I am not sure that he thought of me. Or what he would have thought if he had.

Whatever it was that he was thinking about, it was all cleared from his mind when he felt the boat's power reduce and he heard what he could have sworn were gunshots. When the cargo door opened he hid behind a crate that smelled like olives.

"Mr. Paul," a voice whispered. "Mr. Paul." It was Slamet, the ship's captain. Paul raised his head, and when Slamet saw him, he jogged over to where Paul was hiding.

"Mr. Paul. You come up. Maybe for white man they make the ransom and no kill. If no white man, they kill more. The white man, they ransom only."

"What do you mean? Kill more? Ransom? What the hell is going on up there? Were those gunshots?" Paul asked.

"They kill my man. He try to drop anchor on the boat of them. But they shoot. They kill. My man. He dead now. Please, Mr. Paul. You come. Maybe they ransom," Slamet pleaded.

Paul's instinct was to stay and hide, but he knew it was all his fault. They were after him. He had to take responsibility. Maybe he could save the others. Paul knew his fate had caught up to him. He expected the general himself to greet him with a large gun that would be aimed at his forehead. A gun that had been used to kill many a communist and several recent political opponents. A gun that killed, without regret, men and women who had done much less to offend the general than to murder his only son.

As Slamet led Paul up the stairs and through the heavy door leading to the top deck, the morning light pierced Paul's eyes. He walked, dizzy with a kind of euphoria. He heard voices. They were in a language he'd never heard before.

"They're not Indonesian," Paul said.

"No," Slamet said as a man with an AK-47 walked toward them yelling in this unfamiliar gibberish. "Filipino," Slamet whispered. "The pirates, Mr. Paul."

"Fucking pirates . . ." Paul muttered to himself with the subtlest of grins as the butt of the AK-47 made powerful contact with his skull.

CHAPTER 30

When the small cargo ship, the *Batavia Sedikit*, was officially recovered, there were few signs of the original crew. According to authorities, alerts went out when a suspicious group of locals tried to dock an Indonesian vessel in the port of Cebu with no official manifest and not enough cash for a sufficient bribe. Once the ship was boarded and searched it was clear that foul play had been at hand. Interpol was called in, and while some facts came to light, much speculation was born.

The facts do show that Paul was on the boat at some point. His phone, a pen, and a cocktail napkin with literary scribblings in his handwriting were found in the cargo hull next to a crate of olives. After arrests were made and interrogations took place, it became understood that the entire crew had been shot when Paul attempted to lead a mutiny against the pirates. Reports suggest that he was unconscious on the deck while the pirates debated what to do about him and the rest of the crew. At some point, to their surprise, Paul awoke and leaped up to tackle the pirate closest to him. While the two of them wrestled for the man's rifle, the other pirates fired into Paul's back. Some of the bullets went through and killed the other man as well. Both bodies were stripped and thrown overboard, and the rest of the crew was then executed. Fearing discovery, all of the crew's clothing, after being searched and emptied of valuables, was placed in a garbage bag and also thrown to the sea.

I can imagine Paul in his final moments, narrating in his head what was happening. No doubt, he imagined the scene as he'd describe it in the screenplay, wishfully thinking, even then, that his unfinished novel would be optioned and adapted into a film. He saw the camera moves and might have uttered some sort of foulmouthed remark toward the man he attacked, some valiant phrasing that made use of "the fuck," just to see how it played aloud. Picturing the scene brings me pleasure as much as it brings me heartbreak. Because, knowing Paul, even in a state of such great fear, he would have found a way to observe it all as if seated in a theater. He would have brought some entertainment, some prosaic value, to his final seconds. Which is why it pleases me in the strangest of ways to know that he might have died the dramatic death of his dreams, even if it was decades too soon for my taste.

Before leaving Jakarta, I helped Tetti to handle Paul's belongings. I told her to keep anything she might need. She didn't take much except for a shirt that she said reminded her of Paul. She also kept the kitchen cutlery, which happened to be quite nice. I asked Rahim if he would like anything, and he said that he only wanted the Iron Maiden tape that he and Paul used to listen to. Technically, it was Rahim's tape in the first place, but it was all he asked for.

I took what little else there was and donated it to Paul's friend in the village next to the office. I explained to him as best as I could who Paul was and why Paul would have wanted me to give him these things. He thanked me and said that he wished this man Paul would have come to visit him. Then he embraced me with strong arms as if I were a sister he knew he'd never see again.

Justin and Chan married and moved to Melbourne, Australia, though Justin became Max Rambo's new chief of creative to honor the debt for Chan. He flies to Cambodia to meet Mr. Rambo every few months. They discuss plans and ideas, none of which, Justin says, ever become much of anything, but all of which always excite Mr. Rambo. Chan and I e-mail often and meet on video chat every few weeks. She works at a small coffee shop down the street from where Justin has opened a boutique ad agency. Her English is now at least as good as mine and she tells me she's writing a memoir that she would like me to help edit soon.

Jeff moved to Moscow and works closely with Vadim and Alexis, opening innovative mega-clubs all around the Third World and beyond. I'm in touch with him less often now but he did recently write to tell me that next year they will open a club on an artificial island off the coast of Baja, Mexico, "that will make the Arena Club look like a fucking kids' park." I can't imagine. He insists that I attend the grand opening and plans to fly Justin and Chan in as well.

At the memorial service for Paul in New York, I met many of his friends from New York City as well as from Stonetown, all of whom were as wonderful and fun as Paul had described them to be. I even met the infamous Keri and Rebecca. Rebecca informed me that she had both heroin and angel dust if I wanted, but that she would only give me one or the other and definitely not both.

As all of his peers insisted he would have wanted, there was a legendary after-party. I did not try heroin nor angel dust, but I did have my first experience with MDMA that night, which I found enlightening and revealing, and I subsequently had my first one-night stand. It was with a Stonetown boy who will remain nameless. He was handsome and muscular like an action figure and, as he proudly explained through an inebriated slur, "was put on this earth to drive fast and fornicate."

As the sun was rising and the party was winding down, we went back to his house and when we reached his bedroom I pounced on him like a wildcat. Before my last button was undone I did indeed have my first orgasm. We undressed fully and began again. As I neared my second orgasm, I closed my eyes and pictured Paul fucking me the way a man who battled pirates would fuck. I cried out for Allah and imagined the morning calls to prayer, waves of sound rushing eastward across the Pacific, across time. Paul's body collapsed onto mine with a sweaty splash. I held him tight and licked the moisture from his neck as he whispered things sarcastic and sweet to me through long deep breaths. Inshallah.